ROME

REFRAMED

Amy Bearce

ROME
REFRAMED

a Wish & Wander book

Amy Bearce

JOLLY
FiSH
PRESS
Mendota Heights, Minnesota

First Edition
First Printing, 2021

Book design by Sarah Taplin
Cover design by Sarah Taplin
Cover images by Lisa Kolbasa/Shutterstock; BarbaraALane/Pixabay; SinnesReich/Pixabay

Jolly Fish Press, an imprint of North Star Editions, Inc.

Library of Congress Cataloging-in-Publication Data (pending)
978-1-63163-516-8

Jolly Fish Press
North Star Editions, Inc.
2297 Waters Drive
Mendota Heights, MN 55120
www.jollyfishpress.com
Printed in Canada

To my friends, for all the support

The Palm Reader

Rome, Italy

The Roman palm reader—as she appeared to those around her in this time and place—watched the boy from a distance. He was unaware of everything but the water spilling from the Trevi Fountain. The boy stood at the fountain's edge and wished for home. The woman smelled the wish on the air, more delicious than the spicy scent of tomato sauce from the nearby pizzeria. She smiled and reached into her faded woven bag, the sun reflecting off the heart tattoos along her arm. The coin would have a new owner today.

CHAPTER ONE

The Mystery

Italy was shaped like a boot. No wonder it was kicking my butt. Well, to be fair, it wasn't just Italy. It was the whole six-months-on-the-road-as-a-family thing for my parents' work. The rest of Europe was mostly a blur at this point, but the fountain in front of me now was crystal clear and hard to miss.

The Trevi Fountain hogged most of the street corner where three narrow ancient roads met, with lots of white marble and bright blue water. Some ancient sea god stood front and center. He had a hipster beard and was missing half his clothes, but there was no doubt that this dude was confident and in charge of his fate. Must be nice.

I snapped a photo and reminded myself to jot down the time and date in my school travel journal. The god was Neptune, maybe? Or Oceanus? Most ancient gods looked the same to me. Most big-deal fountains did, too.

Okay, none quite so impressive as this one, true. Rome won the trophy for the best fountain. Still, I'd take the waters of Lake Travis back in Austin anytime.

I wish I could be at home right now.

Just a few more days left of living out of my suitcase. I'd

already lost the second half of my eighth-grade year to this trip, including my last soccer season in middle school. At least I'd have the summer to get back in shape before high school tryouts. I'd been waiting to be on the high school's soccer team since I was nine. But first, I had to get through my last big assignment for my art, history, and English teachers and turn it in before we left.

Did I have any good photos for today yet? I forgot to pay attention half the time during our tours. I scrolled past the Trevi images, a few bronze statues, and eight selfies looking up my nose, before pausing on the close-up of the square toilet seat from yet another café. Yeah, that might be my best shot all week. Kei was going to love that one—for what we called our "European fine art collection."

"Hey, Lucas, who are those guys holding the horses?" my younger brother Robby asked.

I looked up from my photos. Below the sea god boss, two water-horses were plunging through the waves on either side of him, with two helpers holding their reins. One of the horses looked chill, but the one on the right seemed to be freaking out pretty hard.

Robby continued, "The two horses represent the ocean's calm and wild states, but I don't remember the names of the guys holding their reins."

I snorted. "And you think I do?"

Robby always knew stuff like that. He was smarter than most ten-year-olds—and most fourteen-year-olds for that matter—and was always curious.

"They're helping control the god's chariot," I guessed.

Robby did not look convinced. Like I said, he was smart. He'd probably look it up later.

Our little brother Trevor reared back, pawing at the air, and made a sound that was a cross between shrieking and gurgling. "I'm a horse! Like those!"

I gestured at the freaking-out horse and told Trevor, "You look just like him. Good job."

He galloped off to show our parents. Blessed with a moment of quiet, I studied my phone again. Yeah, I'd need some more photos to go with my journal entries. The goofy shot of the bronzed horse butt from this morning would definitely not earn me any points.

My travel journal was supposed to "bring this trip to life." I was writing it old-school in a little notebook and typing everything later on our family laptop, then uploading it with my photos for three of my classes. Not that anyone *really* cared what I thought about Rome. Or Florence. Or Venice. I wasn't anything like my professor parents, getting paid to share their supersmart opinions with other supersmart people.

I'd much rather be playing soccer and eating Texas barbeque at home, but I tried not to think about it too much. Soon everything would go back to the way it used to be.

Robby tugged on my sleeve. "Can we get some gelato now?"

It took my brain a moment to process "gelato" as "ice cream." They weren't the same thing, exactly, but gelato was the Italian word *for* ice cream . . . close enough. My two younger brothers had slipped into this weirdly nomadic life like they were born into it.

I said, "How about when we get back to the bed and breakfast?"

"Can we go back now? Mom and Dad'll be here for hours," Robby said.

Probably true. My parents were busy interviewing tourists and locals throughout Europe to write some thick college book on the histories of big cities around the world.

My mom told us the story a million times of how she'd fallen in love with Rome during a high school trip but believed she'd never get to come back—her dad felt people should bloom where they were planted (sensible guy). But then some kid told her to wish on the Trevi Fountain with a coin and she *knew* she'd come back one day, somehow. Sounds nuts, but the story made her smile every time.

So when she and my dad finally got their book deal, of course they saved Rome for the last and longest stop on their six-month research trip. And it *was* research, not just fun. They took their writing very seriously. Actually, they took everything seriously. They must wonder every day where I came from.

"Five more minutes," I told my brothers. "I need a few more pictures. Don't run away or anything."

"I'm not a baby," Robby snapped. "I'm not going to take off."

"No, but Trevor's only six," I said. Trevor was spinning in circles. "Keep an eye on him." Watching Trevor had pretty much become my job since we started traveling. I didn't mind too much, but today I needed to work.

Robby scowled but grabbed Trevor by the belt loop before he toppled over the edge into the water. Not bad.

I left them sitting on the steps and wandered along the edge of the fountain, studying it again to find a less boring shot. Coins covered the basin of the fountain, wavering beneath the water, mostly euro coins, but there were plenty of quarters in there, too. Dumb. Throwing away perfectly good money had never made sense to me.

"Why don't you make a wish?" The voice at my shoulder made me fumble my phone, and I nearly dropped it in the water.

An old woman stood next to me, smiling. She didn't look like your typical old lady. She had short, spiky white hair streaked with green on one side. Tattoos of hearts marched down one arm. Her tie-dyed dress was so bright it could burn eyes, and a sign hanging around her neck said, "Palm readings: anytime, anyplace!"

"I can't make a wish. I don't have any coins." My hand automatically checked for my wallet in its secure jacket pocket. I'd been warned about pickpockets a thousand times, and a palm reader could definitely fit the bill. She had a thick Italian accent, but her English was clear.

I shook my head. Crook or not, no way would I be throwing away even a small coin. It was only one euro for a scoop of gelato at the shop in our B&B. My brothers ate a lot of gelato.

She smiled.

I was actually surprised this woman spoke to me in English. Lots of little old ladies had struck up conversations with me in Italian the past few weeks. I could barely say a word in Italian beyond *hello, thank you*, and *please*, but maybe I looked at home here. Brown hair, olive skin, and what my mom calls a "Roman nose." She says it's a marker of nobility, but all I know is, it's a honker, and old people kept talking to me in Italian.

The lady held out a coin. "Take this one. Go on, now. It's meant for wishing."

The deep bronze of the metal reflected the sun. It looked hefty. "Where's that from? I've never seen a coin like that before." It wasn't a euro or an American coin. My hands itched to hold it.

She smiled again, and it brought a twinkle to her eye. "Oh, it came from here and there. Much like you these days, eh?"

A chill raced down my back. "What?"

"Your parents are clearly not from here." She gestured to my parents, interviewing a mustached man across the square. My mom wore a backpack, and my dad had on his travel vest holding his fancy recording equipment in the big pockets.

The weird palm reader smiled. "And you've visited all the big tourist sites."

Okay, time to go. Eying my little brothers, I took a step away from the woman. "Yeah, well, speaking of my parents, I'd better go."

She laughed loudly, turning heads across the square. "You're in no danger from me. Here. Take the coin. But you can't keep it. Not this one. Make a wish. To do it right, face away from the fountain, and throw it in the water over your shoulder. You know what they say, don't you? When in Rome, do as the Romans do."

"Yeah, they say that if you throw a coin into the Trevi Fountain, it means you'll return to Rome." *No thanks.*

"*This* coin will empower any wish you want to make. But is Rome really so bad?"

She tapped me lightly on the top of my head. Given that I was a half-foot taller than she was, that took some work. I blinked—*what just happened?*—and she slipped away into a passing crowd of tourists.

The coin flashed in the sun. The ridges were rough against my fingertips. I held it closer, turning it over and back again. It was bronze, with faded writing in some script I'd never seen before that looked like scribbles.

I took a snap of the coin and slipped it into my pocket. Rome wasn't anything like home, and home was the only place I wanted to be.

Two Friends

We headed back for our afternoon break and stopped by the gelato shop like usual. It was on the first floor of our bed and breakfast and had the best gelato in Europe. I took my scoop—I went for the cheesecake and blueberry flavor today and waved at Viviana.

Vivi was always asking questions about America, but she wasn't usually here this early in the day. Her dad, Signor Bonacelli, owned and ran the B&B, including the gelato shop. Trevor found the signore fascinating in part because he'd been born without his left pinky finger, just like Trevor was. What were the odds?

Vivi beamed at me over the ice cream—*gelato*—and with a quick glance at her dad, undid her apron and scurried around the counter. Her curly brown hair was tied back in a low ponytail, but a few curls had escaped around her neck. Her skin was a little deeper olive than mine, and her cheeks were always rosy.

"What did you see for your third-to-last morning in Rome?" she asked, her dark brown eyes snapping with excitement.

Trevor jumped right in, unconcerned about the smooth beard

of melted chocolate gelato on his face. "We saw a FOUNTAIN, a giant, huge fountain with water-horses!"

Robby, though older, was not to be outdone. "We saw a guy playing guitar on the corner, and he was really good."

We did? I must have missed that while I was taking my up-the-nose selfies. Which were, by any objective measure, priceless.

Robby chattered on a bit longer about the guitarist with Trevor trying to interrupt. Man, put a pretty girl in front of them and they babbled like fools. Good thing they had a level-headed bro to look out for them. "Get on upstairs for rest time," I told them. "I'll be up in a minute."

After they left, I pulled out my phone, scrolling backward to the start of the day. "Time for a virtual tour?"

Vivi liked seeing my photos each day, saying she didn't get out much. She was the real reason I started taking more serious shots these last few weeks.

She nodded with a smile but wrinkled her nose at the first picture. "Is that . . . a WC?"

Her accent sounded fancy even when she was saying "WC"—the shorthand for "water closet," which is the polite European way to say *toilet*.

Whoops. I usually pulled those shots out of my main file before seeing her. Clearing my throat, I swiped past it. "It's, uh, for my friend. He's weird."

She raised one eyebrow high, lips quirking. "*He's* weird?"

I shrugged, heat lighting the back of my neck. Aaannnd, there was a horse butt and a statue of some stone naked dude who'd totally lost his private parts, and another dude that looked like it was picking its nose from just the right angle. I'd found the perfect angle.

She snorted—from amusement or disapproval? I was too afraid to look, so I tipped my phone up and frantically scrolled to the normal shots. Finally. I turned my screen to her.

"Ah, the Trevi Fountain," she nodded knowingly. "Oceanus, the sea god. Nice choice."

Oceanus. I needed to add that to my notes. "We did the Colosseum this morning, too. Guess I forgot to take any pictures there but this one from the outside." *Dang it.*

"How was it? I hear it's very crowded."

"Wait, you haven't been?" I practically had to scoop myself off the floor. She lived so close to it but hadn't gone to see such a famous place?

"Not since I was little—I don't even remember it. And I was sick the day my class went as a school trip." She shrugged. "I don't mind. It's mostly for tourists."

"That's me." I laughed.

"What's that coin?" she asked, peering closer as she swiped through the shots.

"Good question." A quick snap of static electricity zapped my fingertips as I pulled the coin out of my pocket. "Have you ever seen something like this? Is it from ancient Rome?"

She examined it and shook her head. "I don't know what it is. Did you find it?"

"Someone gave it to me. A lady I've never met before."

She blinked, handing back the ancient coin. "That's a bit odd, isn't it?"

Despite the oddity, the mystery of the coin clearly didn't interest Vivi much. She leaned forward on the counter and returned to our travel discussion with glowing eyes. "You've seen so much over the last six months! What's been your favorite so far? Out of everywhere you've gone?"

She sounded eager, like she was living a little through me.

"What, like, a favorite place out of all of Europe?"

She nodded. "We're so close to so many other countries, but we rarely even leave the city. The B&B keeps us too busy."

Hmm. "Well, I liked Germany. Their doner kebabs were fantastic. The pancake soup in Bavaria was, too, which sounds disgusting but was amazing. But then again, Switzerland had seriously delicious goulash." Swapping the coin back for my phone, I found my shot of the steaming bowl and showed her.

"Food seems to be a theme with you." She giggled.

"Best part of traveling." I wasn't even joking. "Nobody can beat Rome's pasta. Or gelato." I even used the right word.

Dimples flashed in her cheeks with her smile. "Where did you go yesterday?"

I had to pause and scroll through a few more pictures to remind myself. "Oh yeah, we did the National Roman Museum yesterday, and the Pope's place."

We bent our heads together over my phone. I didn't have as many photos as I should, but there were a few. She pointed to a picture of the Vatican, the light streaming all around it. "You have a good eye, Lucas. Are you going to be an artist when you grow up? A photographer?"

I studied the picture and stifled a grin. Huh. It wasn't bad, I guess—the way the light came in, it made the whole thing more interesting. I hearted it to remind myself to use it in my journal. "I don't know what I want to do. I like a lot of things."

"Like what?"

My gelato was melting, so I took a bite while I thought. "I like soccer, but I don't think I'm good enough to be pro." I shrugged.

"Do you want to write like your parents?"

"I'm not exactly great at writing." My fifth-grade English teacher, Ms. Anderson, would say that was the understatement of the year. "Plus, it's too hard for too little money."

I jerked my chin toward my dad, who was crouched in the corner, hunched over his laptop, clacking away like a maniac. I mean, he was never the kind of dad who'd kick around a soccer ball with me—he's not exactly the athletic type—but until last year, he actually had time to watch a movie or do a puzzle with us (yes, puzzles were popular in my family) when he wasn't teaching at the university. Mom, too. They used to get on my case a lot about my grades not being so hot, but since the book deal, they'd been working 24-7.

"Well, I think you should do what you love." Her voice grew stronger. "You've got a gift with images, with photographs. You should use it!"

I studied the shot. Was it really good? The only thing I'd ever felt good at was soccer and making people laugh.

I lifted my spoon. "Right now, I'm thinking the real gift is this gelato."

She giggled. See? A guy's gotta work with what he's got.

"You could always own a gelato shop," she teased. "Though you might eat all your wares."

We both laughed. My phone chimed a reminder that Kei and I had a video chat scheduled soon. I checked the time. It felt so much later in the day when you started touristing at the break of dawn with travel-obsessed parents. "Hey," I asked. "It's early for you to be home, isn't it?" I normally saw her only after dinner. "Y'all have school on Fridays, right?"

Wiping down the already-clean counter, she said, "Today and Monday, students are on holiday while the teachers have a training for a new program. It's an unusual break for us."

I nodded. "Nice. My school year actually finishes in a week. Then we have the summer off. Though at this rate, I'll still be working on my last journal assignment until I'm eighteen."

She gave a deep sigh. "One day, I'll make a travel journal, too. Only mine will be from all over the world, especially America."

"You can come visit me anytime." The words just fell out of my face without planning. My cheeks warmed. What if she thought I was flirting? *Was* I flirting? No. Luckily, she seemed to take me at face value.

"That's sweet of you, Lucas. I'm glad your family chose our B&B. I hate that you're leaving already so soon. I hear Americans are impatient, so maybe that's why." She laughed.

She's not the only one who thinks Americans are all

impatient. There are a few ideas about Americans that seem to be everywhere.

According to international stereotypes (what, as if we don't have plenty about other countries?), Americans are

1. Loud.
2. Obnoxious.
3. Lovers of ugly white tennis shoes.
4. Uncouth.

Uncouth. What do they know?

Vivi had to work, so I headed up to my room and sent the horse's crack, the nose pick, and the square toilet seat to Kei. He'd get a laugh out of those. I even added in some agonized angel faces from a mausoleum that looked like examples of demented torture techniques.

I worked on homework until about one-ish, just after lunch. That made it six a.m. in Texas, and Kei had said he'd call before school. Time zones are weird.

I sat at the laptop, waiting. Pulling out the coin, I set it next to the laptop to show him.

1:10.

1:15.

1:25.

I double-checked our last message. Yeah, he said he'd call Friday morning whenever he was done getting ready. He'd missed the last time and said he'd definitely call today. He'd bought a new game he wanted to talk about.

I sent a video chat request, but there was no answer.

1:30.

By now, he'd be getting on the bus. He wasn't calling.

There were lots of reasons he might not have called or even bothered answering when I did. Maybe he wasn't feeling good. Maybe he had homework to finish before school.

Or maybe he just forgot.

You know what they say—out of sight, out of mind.

CHAPTER THREE

The Wish

Mashing my lips tight, I closed the laptop's cover. So a friend didn't call. That was okay. I'd be home soon, and then everything would go back to how was. It would be *fine*.

Then Trevor started puking—the lactose intolerant dude ate too much gelato so that put a halt on the afternoon excursion. Robby was disappointed, but I shrugged. It wasn't like I wanted to squeeze in another fountain or statue. After the rest of today, I just had to get through Saturday and Sunday, really. We'd leave Monday at lunch. I couldn't wait to get home.

"Have you written your entry today?" my mom asked, pointedly.

No. I sighed, pulling out my little notebook. The blank page might as well be a black hole. I didn't have anything to say, and since we stayed in this afternoon, now I'd have even less material to work with. The shots from this morning still weren't enough.

I scrolled through my earlier photos. We'd gone to the Vatican Museums and St. Peter's Basilica. Then there was the day at Pompeii, and the Roman Forum before that. There weren't that many pictures, though, and they all looked like a typical tourist brochure. It kinda explained my last few not-so-hot grades on my city projects.

I wondered how Ms. Deblasio felt about weird toilets and horse butts.

The coin on the desk drew my gaze. I guess I could write about *that*. Opening up my laptop again, I searched online but couldn't find anything about it. There wasn't a minting location or a date printed on it, either. Maybe it had been worn away.

After examining it again, I tossed it on the desk. There was something about that coin, something unusual that made me want to keep it close. I put it back in my pocket. I focused again on the page and writing about Roman art and history, which led to me taking a quick nap. Naps were one of my strongest skills.

For dinner, we didn't even eat out, just grabbed some quick sandwiches at a food cart down the street. My dad got an espresso, which is like a tiny cup of super-bitter, intense coffee. I never understood the appeal of espresso even though it was very popular here. But the sandwiches were awesome, like most of the food in Italy.

Now granted, it wasn't a sour cream chicken enchilada from Garcia's, my top meal ever, with cheesy, oozy goodness. But my salami and cheese sandwich was still really great. My salami breath afterward was *not* great, though. If Kei had been here, I'd breathe on him and make him gag. I snickered at the thought.

"What's so funny?" Robby asked.

He'd bug me until I answered him. Resistance was futile.

"I was thinking of the last time I spent the night at Kei's and he Dutch-ovened me, but I got him back later with my breath."

He tilted his head sideways like a confused puppy. "What's a Dutch oven?"

"Oh come on, you know!"

When he looked at me blankly, I shook my head. I was clearly failing in my big brother duties. He was already ten—he should know this stuff. Book smarts weren't everything. "It's when you fart under the covers, and then pull them over someone's head and keep them in there with the fumes."

He squinched up his face and glared at me. "That's so gross!" Then he pulled his blanket tight around him on his tiny cot of a bed.

I laughed again. "You'll see one day. Go to bed, Second of the Offspring."

His glare grew deeper. "I'm not sleepy."

"If you go to bed, I won't do this to you all night." I leaned over and huffed my salami breath on him.

"Stop it, you nerd! Gross!" Robby smacked me with his book but didn't gag.

"Ow!" I rubbed my arm, kinda proud of him. His book had fallen in my lap. *Landmarks of Italy*. I pointed at it. "You're calling *me* a nerd?"

"You're just jealous that I know so much."

"That's what you think." I gave him a noogie and ignored the sting just under my chest bone. I was used to comments like that—I had a nice callus built up there. He *was* smarter than me.

Lots. He made straight As and studied for fun. That was our family's motto, pretty much.

We didn't have much in common, but he wasn't bad for a little brother.

"Boys!" My dad stood at the doorway, wiping off his glasses. "Can you keep it down?"

Things got quiet after that. Car horns floated through my open window, along with faint music and the chatter of crowds. There was no air-conditioning, like most places here, and the air always felt heavier and smelled like not-home. But the light in the apartment was cozy, yellow and warm.

The clock read 10:35 p.m. when ringing sounded from my computer screen. I jumped at the unexpected noise but managed to click ACCEPT CALL.

The screen opened, and Kei appeared. Relief made me smile, and then shock had my jaw dropping. Kei had changed his hair.

I said, "Hey jerk-face. What's up with the hair?"

Kei had bleached the top layer of his normally smooth black hair a yellow blond. Then I got it. "Ah, I see. Like Honda, huh?" I pointed to the wall behind my friend.

A poster of Keisuke Honda, the Japanese soccer player, decorated the wall next to his closet. Honda wore his hair bleached on top, too. Kei totally hero-worshipped the guy. He was a star player, for sure, and they shared first names.

Kei ran a hand through his newly bleached layer, black hair shining through from the bottom. "Figured it'd be good luck for the district game—it worked, too."

"Did your parents freak out?" I asked. Kei's parents were really traditional in a lot of ways.

"Amazingly, nah. Think they've given up on me at this point. Sorry about this morning, man. Overslept. You know how that goes. How ya been? Met any hot Italian girls yet?" He wiggled his eyebrows.

I glanced over my shoulder where my little brothers were sleeping. "Dude, no."

"Talked to that girl Vivi more, though, right?"

I sighed. "Yeah, but it's not like that. I did meet a weird lady today, though. A really strange one." I told him about the coin and held it up for him to examine.

He whistled. "That's got to be ancient. I wonder if it's worth a lot? You could buy a plane ticket home even sooner! Though three days is almost no time, right?"

When I took in my next breath, my lungs felt bigger. Everything was going to be fine.

He snapped his fingers. "And check it—at the end-of-the-year assembly, the whole soccer team got brought up and was given special trophies for being the first team from our school to win district." He pulled a little trophy off his shelf and posed with it like a superstar.

"Wow, that's awesome!" I followed the school's athletic department online and knew Kei had scored a lot. He'd been working really hard. He was probably better than me by now.

A clatter behind Kei had him spinning in his seat. "Oh, hey Brett!"

Brett Sanders appeared behind Kei, waving. I gave a weak wave back.

"Hey, we've got a history project of our own to do, so I've gotta go. But it's good to see you, man." Kei was already looking away, laughing about something with Brett.

"Yeah, talk to you later," I said faintly, but Kei cut the connection before I finished my sentence.

I stared at the blank screen, feeling blank inside myself.

Kei just blew me off for Brett Sanders. Brett Sanders, who used to chew his hair and laughed like a hyena.

They'd probably help each other get ready for soccer tryouts, too. It was tough to make the high school team. They were probably already having scrimmages with others from our middle school team to prepare.

While I was stuck here.

Thanks to my parents' trip, I was missing the awesome annual eighth-grade trip to the NASA Space Center in Houston, the eighth-grade graduation ceremony (kinda hokey but a big traditional moment), and most importantly, the *entire* soccer season of my last year at McKinney Middle School.

Soccer was really popular in Europe, but I never had a time or place to practice, what with all the touristing. It put me at a big disadvantage for trying out for the high school team in November.

I'd tried to tell my parents, but they didn't understand. I couldn't believe I missed such a good season, too. It would have been my first award at a school assembly other than for perfect attendance. But the team deserved the recognition, especially Kei.

The room suddenly felt way too small. I needed to move. Staying stuffed up in old buildings all day worked for my family, but not for me. My feet felt itchy, with zips of energy racing up and down my legs. Going for a run sounded like the best idea I'd ever had. When I got back to Texas, I wanted to be able to jump right into my life like I'd never left, and that meant I *had* to make the freshman soccer team.

Suddenly, nothing had ever felt so important.

I poked my head into my parents' tiny bedroom of our apartment suite. "Hey, I need to take a quick jog. Just down to the Trevi and back."

Mom looked up from her laptop with bleary eyes. "Okay, but be careful. It's late. Keep your passport tucked in your waist belt, and don't stay too long. We've got plans early in the morning."

Of course we did. There was never any time to just breathe. For them, it was easy to learn stuff really fast. To me, multiple tours in a day felt like an information fire hose to the face.

I set off at an easy pace, settling into the rhythm of my run. Lights from the street lit my path. Each pound of my shoes was another word: *I'll. Be. Home. Soon. I'll. Be. Home. Soon.*

And then everything would be like it used to be.

Even this late, there were crowds in the streets, along with the general hum that came from lots of people, just like in Paris, London, and Berlin. The weather here in May was perfect, especially in the evenings, with a kind of crisp warmth that I'd miss when we went home. Maybe the *only* thing I'd miss.

My mind flashed to Vivi smiling, and my steps stumbled. Then I kept jogging.

For the first time, I wasn't sure what it would be like when I got back home. Even if Kei and I both made the soccer team, would he even still want to hang out next year? What if I didn't make the team? I'd end up without anyone to hang with, even at home.

Why did things have to be so complicated?

The sound of rushing water echoed down the narrow street, leading me to the large landmark. The base of the fountain was actually below street level, set up like a mini-amphitheater, with several rows of steps leading down from the center path to the fountain itself.

Catching my breath, I headed down the steps and walked along the edge of the fountain, letting the splashing sounds of the water soothe me. The fountain looked even more impressive at night, all lit up in the darkness.

On the other side of the fountain, two guys about my age were balancing on the basin's edge. They were shoving back and forth like they would knock each other in, but their laughter echoed across the small square. They were clearly best friends and moved in that carefree way that spoke of being completely at home, both in their city and in their own skin. They probably never felt lonely or like big ol' losers.

My throat felt raw, my skin felt too tight. Jamming my fingers in my pockets, my fingers brushed the coin. I gripped it, as if I could hold onto my past that way.

On a whim, I faced the fountain I wasn't going to do it over my shoulder—the proper Roman way, just in case—and made a wish: *I want to go back. I want to be at home.*

I threw the coin into the water. *Plunk!* The water was so shallow that I could count every coin. The big coin from the strange lady sat right on top of the pile, glittering in the blue glow of the fountain's lights.

A second later, I plunged my hand into the cool water and pulled out my coin, ignoring the "Hey!" and "Watch it!" from people around me. One touristy-looking lady even yelled, "That's illegal!" Shoving away from the fountain, I wiped the coin on my shirt and pocketed it. The lady stomped off in a huff, but I didn't care.

It's not like wishing ever made something happen, and this coin was one of the most interesting things that had happened to me here. Sad but true. I would squeeze out a paragraph for my school journal about the coin somehow. My work had been low quality lately even for me, and *something* had to fill it up. I'd write more about the Trevi, too. Heaven knows I'd seen it enough times to draw it from memory. It would have to be enough. I opened my little notebook right there on the stairs and scribbled my entry. I'd type it all up later, before we left.

Dear Ms. Morris, Ms. Deblasio, and Mr. Franklin,

Today I visited the Trevi Fountain. It's one of the most famous fountains in Rome. You can hear the water from pretty far away. At the center is a big god. I thought at first it was Neptune with his tritons. But I learned from a friend here that it's Oceanus. The two water horses are supposed to show how the ocean can be both calm and stormy.

There are lots of coins in the fountain. It's tradition that if you toss a coin over your shoulder, you'll return to Rome. My mom did it when she was my age and says that's why we came back. I think we came back because my parents wanted to write a book about history and this place has a lot of it.

Anyway, the city collects the fountain coins every night and gives them to a charity, which is nice. I tried out the tradition with this special coin I was given, but changed my mind and grabbed it out. Rome is nice, but I'd rather not come back. Apparently, it's illegal to remove a coin from the fountain, but that's okay. I won't be making any more wishes anyway.

Sincerely,

Lucas

After all that, I couldn't settle down. The gelato shop closed soon, but maybe I had time to grab a late-night snack. I missed having a kitchen.

I entered through the inside hall, since the B&B was

connected. Vivi was at the counter, alone for once. Her dad must be cleaning in the back, from the sounds of the pots clanging. As she wiped down the counter, she sang under her breath in Italian. Her singing made me want to lean in and listen, but when saw me, she stopped mid-note, with a little jump. "Lucas! You startled me!"

"Sorry!" I waved, hoping I looked casual and not like a creepy stalker. "Since when do you work so late?"

She straightened her apron. "We're open later on Friday, Saturday, and Sunday, and we're really short-staffed right now. Papa's locking up soon. Why are you out so late?"

Pointing at the gelato, I said, "Well, I went running and was hoping for one last scoop tonight."

"Sure. What would you like?" she asked, holding the scooper ready. "The weirdest flavor we have, like usual?"

I couldn't help but smile back at her mischievous grin. "That sounds like a challenge." On a whim, I asked, "What do you recommend? What's your favorite?"

She blinked. "You haven't asked me that, not once in three weeks."

Huh. She was right. "Well that's dumb of me. Which should I choose? You definitely have—haha—the *inside scoop* on the best flavors."

She half laughed, half groaned at the bad pun—her English was great. "Chocolate."

I hooted. "*Chocolate?* Plain ol' chocolate?"

She lifted her nose, looking perfectly prissy. "It's better than all the fancy flavors you're always eating. Try it for yourself."

She dropped one scoop into a bowl, my preferred gelato delivery device. I took a spoonful and allowed it to melt on my tongue, closing my eyes to savor it.

Rich. Bitter. Sweet. All at the same time.

When I opened my eyes, she was smiling with one eyebrow raised. "I'm right, yes?"

I laughed. "You know you are."

She tidied up as I finished my scoop. She didn't sing this time, but the silence was comfortable somehow.

"Quiet out tonight," she commented. "Comparatively. A nice almost-last night in Rome for you, I guess."

"Yep. Three days—no, two and a half—and we'll be on our way home. Hardly any time left here at all." Then this little shop and everything in it would be in my past. A little dart of disappointment hit me, surprising me.

Vivi's father came in, giving me a once-over. "Hello, Lucas. You are out late."

"Yes sir, just heading upstairs after a quick snack," I said, tossing my trash. I glanced at Vivi. "We're going out early to beat the crowds tomorrow."

Vivi nodded. "I'll be at breakfast. See you then?"

Signor Bonacelli gave me steely eyes, like she'd asked me on a date or something, jeez. It was worthy of an eye roll, but I kept a smile plastered on to be polite.

"Sure." I gave a half-wave, half-salute—*smooth, Lucas*—and clomped upstairs.

In my room, I set out my clothes for tomorrow. My things had managed to scatter around the space in the last three weeks, almost like I really lived here. I stuffed most of it back in my suitcase.

As I lay there that night trying to sleep and failing, a thought popped in my head: When we left, would Vivi expect a hug goodbye? Maybe just a wave. A handshake? I shook my head at myself. I was such a dork. But it wasn't every day I got to chat with an Italian friend. And I was pretty sure we counted as friends at this point.

I fell asleep with a smile on my face.

In the morning, when my alarm went off, I woke up in a good mood. My email had a new alert—maybe Kei sent me something—and I went to open it.

It was from my history teacher, along with my English teacher, and art teacher, all the ones who were grading my city journal projects. I frowned. The subject line said, "Concerns."

My stomach did a slow turn, and I hesitated just for a moment before clicking.

My eyes scanned their letter fast. Then I read it again. *No.* My lungs squeezed hard. My breath wheezed out.

Dear Lucas,

We regret to inform you that your last project, about Florence, does not qualify for a passing score. The descriptions of your sightseeing were minimal and perfunctory. Your photos were either basic, blurry, or absent. You included nothing about your last day at all. This is not the first time you've sent work at this level.

We spoke together and agreed that this time, this project will receive an F. You cannot make this up, as you are no longer in Florence. Unfortunately, this pulls your grade in all of our classes below passing. But if you make an A on your Rome project by doing a truly excellent job, you can still pass our classes with a C and therefore promote to high school. We hope you will seriously consider this.

Let us be painfully clear: if you do not pass our classes, you will not pass eighth grade. Review the City Journal requirements. We have included your parents on this email.

Sincerely,

Ms. Morris, Ms. Deblasio, and Mr. Franklin

I collapsed into the desk chair, knees too weak to hold me. *No.*

Failing eighth grade? Not going to high school next year at all? Being left behind entirely? Let everyone see what I already knew and had kept hidden: that I wasn't smart enough to pass?

An F!

F for failure.

Fail.

CHAPTER FOUR
The Challenge

My feet paced me around the room while my brain took off at a thousand miles an hour.

There had to be a way to fix this. Sitting, I reread their letter. They'd included an attachment at the end. A rubric! A reminder of what they wanted from me! I'd had it from the start but never really looked at it again since a quick glance on Day 1. But today I scoured it.

City Journal Assignment for Mr. Franklin (English),
Ms. Deblasio (Art) and Ms. Morris (History):

For every city you visit, please construct daily journal entries and photos, submitted online before you leave that city. Each day must be accounted for.

In your journal entries, connect emotions, thoughts, and ideas to the city's art, architecture, and history. Make it personal! Facts are fine, but we can look up facts about any of these places and already know quite a bit—we want to know what you think as you experience them, how you feel, and what kinds of questions you have. Share what you learn during tours in your own words.

For Mr. Franklin, write at least one poem within your entries per city. Writing two poems per city journal earns extra credit. Use figurative language.

Photos are required for Ms. Deblasio's art class. Your photos should reflect elements of art as discussed in the textbook: composition, lighting, color balance, etc. Unique perspectives earn more points.

Questions to consider as you write:

What does the history of an area mean in light of today?

What can you tell us that's unique or not commonly known?

How does the art and history you're encountering make you feel and why?

In summary:

Document what you notice, and try to capture how you feel through your shots and journal entries. This requires paying attention and taking your time.

Well, time was *exactly* what I didn't have. But one thing was for sure: I couldn't leave Rome without trying my best to make the most amazing journal project of all time. The thing was . . . they wanted me to rip out my heart and drip blood all over the page for them, but I wasn't sure I even had enough heart to do that.

Regardless, I had to get started right away—before my mother woke up, read that email, and killed me on the spot. My professor parents might die of mortification from having to tell people their oldest kid failed eighth grade. The thought sent my legs scrambling.

I couldn't go far by myself, but luckily, a famous fountain was very close by. I'm sure I could include more about it.

Sweating, I left a note for my parents: "Hi Mom and Dad! I'm heading to the Trevi for more shots! Don't worry!" Maybe they wouldn't check their email first thing. A guy could hope.

It didn't take long for me to reach the Trevi Fountain. How many times had I passed it in the last three weeks? Too many to count.

Ugh. So crowded already. Wasn't Saturday Mass a thing? They had St. Peter's right nearby, for Pete's sake. Mental note: use that line in my journal. Humor was the only thing I had going for me.

I plopped my butt on the steps in front of the fountain and stared at the giant sculptures, opening to a fresh page of my pocket-sized spiral notebook. I'd already said plenty about the Trevi, in my opinion, but I guess they wanted me to wring myself dry here.

How did I let my grades get this bad? Sure, my report card always looked like an eye-test chart instead of straight As. Plenty of Cs and Ds . . . an occasional F, admittedly, though never on the final average for the year. But to totally fail?

If I weren't here, I'd be passing, like always, going to tutoring under the radar if I had to. But this trip was too distracting, provided too much overload. Too much for a guy like me to absorb by myself.

But surely I could pull it together enough for one stupid

project. I'd just write a lot about how amazing everything was. Starting with this freaking huge fountain. I could do this.

My pen was slick in my hands.

That page was really blank.

The water glittered in the sun. People pushed past me, unconcerned about some kid's entire future falling apart.

I pressed my pen to the paper. *Think, Lucas, think.*

The air smelled like somebody's over-confident cologne, but that wasn't the fountain's fault. The sparkles on the water were pretty, kinda like diamonds.

I wrote that down. Could be poetic, sort of? I needed more history, though. What had Robby said about this fountain yesterday? He spouted more facts than this thing did water, but it went in one ear and out the other for me, like my skull was Swiss cheese, full of holes.

Jeez, was this the best I could do? Trevor could do better than this at six. And of course, my parents literally taught people who were already supersmart. Who knew how I ended up in this family?

This was why I didn't bother "doing my best." My best wasn't good enough. I'd hid that for years, but my secret was about to come out.

Groaning, I scribbled across the page.

A voice came at my back. "You seem frustrated."

My pen clattered to the black cobblestones. I picked it up and shaded my eyes. A flash of silver and green reflected in the light.

That lady.

The weirdo lady with the coin was here again. She waved at me. Her heart tattoos flashed in the sunlight, and her rainbow tie-dyed dress nearly blinded me.

"Want to step into my office?" She gestured at a little table set up to one side of the fountain with a sign that read, *Palm Reading: Know Your Future, Change Your Path.*

I looked around, but she was definitely talking to me. The woman grinned at me as I stood, ready to back far, far away.

"Ready for a palm reading?" she asked. "Free for you!" Her Italian accent sounded fancy, with rolling R's and trills.

"Uh, no, thanks. I'm a little busy." *Busy trying not to have a panic attack right here in the square.*

She narrowed her eyes. "Show me your palm. It will tell me what I need to know to help you."

I gestured at the fountain. "I just—"

"Now, please." Her words allowed for no debate. Maybe she went to the same mom school my mother did.

I sighed and flung out my hand.

She held one finger above the line from my thumb to my wrist. "See, here, you've got an artist's heart. The soul of a poet. You hide it, though." She tsked. "There's no shame in it, young man."

Heat flooded my face. Artist? Poet? Um, no. I tugged my hand, but she tightened her grip. Jeez, this lady might tear my hand off. Maybe she wasn't so harmless after all.

"And this line here? By your ring finger? It means you're

in some trouble. Failing at something important to you." She met my eyes.

I gasped. How did she know that? If she was a con artist, she was a good one.

"Rome will help you succeed at this thing you need to do."

"Rome?"

"The city, yes. Mother Rome. She's taken a fancy to you." She winked.

This was too weird. "Uh. Thanks?" I jammed my hands in my pockets and brushed across the coin. No way did I want anything of this freaky lady. "Here's your coin back, by the way. Thanks for the chance to look at it." I held out the coin in my hand.

The woman shook her finger. "Oh, no. You'll need that coin. For a few trips, shall we say?"

Yeah, she was clearly missing a few scoops of gelato.

"I've taken plenty of trips the last six months."

"Yes, but Rome knows you need to see more to have your eyes opened."

My scalp prickled. Maybe she was playing some kind of game with me, a game that would end with all my stuff being stolen. I scowled.

"I've seen lots of Rome. And other places." I flapped my hand at my blank journal. "My eyes are plenty open. I'm just not good at writing stuff, that's all. I'm an athlete, not a brainiac or an artist."

"You can do more than you give yourself credit for. But Rome will make that clear." She handed me two tickets.

They were for the Colosseum—and these said SKIP THE LINE—ALL ACCESS. I'd never seen any tickets like them. Yesterday we'd waited in a line long enough for me to get gray hairs and wrinkles. I'd somehow still managed to only take one photo there, the standard one out front.

"I can't take these, plus I've already been."

"But you didn't really *see* it. Take your Roman friend, the one who's given you many *sweet* experiences. Here's a second chance. And three days, or even two, is not much time, considering all of Rome's vast history, Lucas Duran."

Chills coated me, and I fell back a step like she'd punched me. I'd never told her my name. Had this lady been *spying* on me?

I shook my head and reached for words but found none. Instead, my shaky legs turned and ran, taking the rest of me with them.

She called after me, "Don't forget to take plenty of pictures. Your teachers will like what you have to say after this tour, I think!" Her cackle chased me out of the square.

My fingers stayed clamped on the tickets. My sneakers slapped the cobblestoned streets all the way back to the B&B, my lungs squeezing and wheezing.

Vivi was at the front counter again. As soon as she saw me, her eyes grew wide. "Lucas! What's wrong!"

"There's a lady—she knew my name—I'm failing my class and she knew—heart tattoos—Rome—gave me these—said to take my Roman friend and I think she meant you—sweet things—" I collapsed in a chair, holding out the tickets.

She brought me a glass of water and said firmly, "Breathe and then tell me again. Slowly."

I spilled the story. She studied the tickets, and her eyes began to sparkle.

"Well, then. It sounds like I get to play tourist. If you want the company, I mean."

I couldn't imagine spending all morning with Vivi. We were chat-in-public friends, but not hang-out-for-hours-together friends. What would we talk about the whole time? Would I even have anything to say? Especially being in such a bad mood like I was.

But I couldn't admit any of those worries. "I was just there with my family. Why would this lady care if we go there today?" I asked instead.

"Maybe she was just being nice!"

I shook my head. "These tickets had to cost a lot. No way will my parents let me use them. Especially with just the two of us. Besides, they're going to be too busy freaking out about my grade to even hear what I have to say about this."

At her raised eyebrows, I gave her the quick rundown on the bad news this morning. I didn't mention that failing my project meant *flunking my entire grade*. A guy had his pride.

Her lips quirked. "Well then. It seems luck has found you. You need more details for your journal. This woman has gifted you a way to go back to what you didn't pay attention to the first time. If I go with you, I can ask the staff for some neat little-known facts, in Italian."

"But she knew my name—how creepy is that?"

She huffed. "So maybe don't mention that part to your parents!"

"Vivi!" I gaped at her.

Who was this girl? She'd seemed so quiet at first, but she was full of surprises. Next, she'd probably tell me she had a tattoo. "Are you suggesting I . . . lie?"

She blushed. "No, I'm suggesting we *take advantage* of a once-in-a-lifetime chance to see a world-famous site and save your project while we're at it. It could be fun!"

Actually, it wasn't all that fun to be around an upbeat, cheery person when you felt like garbage. Ever tried it? Super annoying. And yet . . . Vivi somehow got away with it. She was being downright chipper right now, but I couldn't resent it. She was a cool person and was obviously jazzed about going. And she'd know lots of stuff about Italy.

I still didn't get why this palm-reader lady would care, or drag Vivi into all this, but whatever, as long as I passed. "Sure, we can do that. *If* our parents agree."

She squealed and clapped her hands.

Of course, no way would my parents agree to me running around with a friend after they read the email, but at least now when I faced them, I had a plan to offer. And then after they said no, I could hopefully talk them into letting me go to the Colosseum alone, with one of these tickets. It would seem way less fun and therefore more appropriately studious, given the situation. Either way, I'd be better off than now.

Vivi headed up to her apartment, and I straightened my shoulders before entering mine.

My parents were waiting for me, laptops open to the email.

"Well?" My mom said, jerking a thumb at the screen.

Wincing, I spoke calmly but fast. "I'm sorry, okay? I didn't realize I'd done such a bad job."

My mother looked at me like I had an alien popping out of my forehead. "You're *sorry?* We bring you to Europe and you play games on your phone instead of paying attention and—"

My dad thankfully interrupted. "Lucas, we just don't understand. If you tried half as hard on your essays as you did on your soccer skills, you'd be a straight-A student!"

I snorted. "I think you're taking a trip down a certain river in Egypt."

They looked at me blankly.

Sighing, I said, "The Nile? DENIAL? Get it?"

My dad jammed his glasses back on his nose so hard it probably left a mark.

Robby hurried past to the bathroom, head down. He stage-whispered, "Not the time for jokes, Lucas."

My mother said with a growl, "Your brother is correct."

Gee, what a surprise! "Okay, maybe I *could* do better. Right now, I've got to collect enough information and write enough to get an A. Then I'll pass!"

"What about summer school?" my mom asked, running a hand through her hair, voice slightly calmer. "If you fail, surely you could make up the credits and still go to high school?"

Relief mixed with horror. *Summer school? After museums and cathedrals for six months?* "Maybe? They didn't say. But I'd rather not."

My dad shook his head. "Summer school should not be necessary, not after three weeks of living amongst history here, not to mention the last six months of travel!" He gestured at me with his glasses. "You've just got to sit down and write."

I cringed. "Honestly, I didn't really take good notes the last few days"—my mom threw up her arms in frustration—"but Vivi agreed to take me to the Colosseum today if her dad will let her. She'll give me a real Italian tour. My teachers will eat that up with a spoon!" I waited for their *no*, mostly thankful already. No one else needed to watch me agonize over every word I'd have to write.

A laugh burst from my mom, but it was not a funny sound. "You think you're going to go tooling around Rome with a *friend*? You should be grounded!"

Yep. It was all going perfectly according to my plan, such as it was. Lifting my palms in surrender, I said, "True. I don't deserve to go with a friend. But I can't pass my class from inside my room. I've got to make Rome come alive for my project, and that means getting out there, taking notes this time, and taking good photos. My art teacher said stock photos won't count, and she'll know if I use them, too. I could go by myself—that would be painful and full of suffering, so there's that." *And then I could frown all I wanted to.*

"Offspring the First has a point." My dad tried to lighten the mood with his silly nick-name for me. "Maybe he could even take Offspring the Second and Third with him."

"No way," I said, quickly. "I can't take good notes and keep an eye on Robby and Trevor!"

Robby stuck his head through the doorway. "Hey! I could help you with your project!"

I sighed. "You're sick of sightseeing."

"No, that's you," Robby said, jutting out his chin. I knew that look. He was revving up to be a major pain. He was really good at it, too.

I thought fast and said, "It's my project, buddy. I'm not supposed to use other people's thoughts, just my own." Which was all true, as far as it went.

He jerked his face away and stomped back to his room. Trevor's high-pitched voice asked, "What's going on, Robby?"

Robby responded sharply. "Nothing. That's exactly what's going on for us."

His frustration came through loud and clear. I felt bad, but not bad enough to bring them along. Not today. I needed to work, and besides, the palm reader was so weird. What if that lady followed me? A shiver ran down my spine. I'd need to be really careful.

A heartbeat passed while my mother chewed her lip. My dad had already opened his laptop, but Mom pulled him over to whisper together in a quick huddle.

When they broke, my dad rubbed the bridge of his nose under his glasses. "You know, we did have a few other plans today, Lucas. We don't have that much time left in the Eternal City as a family."

Mom glanced at him, then at me. "But, truthfully, your dad and I could use some time this morning to consolidate our notes and meet a deadline with our editor, so . . ."

They exchanged another long parent-glance in their secret parent-glance language. Dad said, "So you can do this, but just for the morning, understood?"

I pumped my fist just as my mom added, "And only if you take Vivi. I know she rides the Metro often, so I trust she'll get you there and back in one piece. Check back here after lunch."

Wait, what? All morning with the bubbly, supersmart Vivi, after all? My knees didn't seem to want to hold me, so I sat down. "Um, are you sure about Vivi? Because—"

"It's the only way I'll approve this. She at least knows her way around the city and speaks the language." Her jaw was set.

I hadn't seen that coming, but Mom had a point. "Oookay, then! I promise I'll use my time better."

Dad said, "I'm confident you will."

No idea why he was so confident, but I'd take it.

"But what about tickets?" asked Mom. "You should pay for Vivi's, too, since she's doing you a huge favor. I think you should have to cover both tickets with your allowance, since we already paid for it once."

I coughed into my fist. True, I hadn't been the most cooperative travel companion the last few weeks. Or months. But in my defense, they'd dragged me here against my wishes, and one old building starts to look a lot like another after six months.

"Um. The tickets are already taken care of." I held my breath, not willing to straight-up lie, but as I hoped, they just nodded absent-mindedly, probably just glad to not have to fork over any more money on something they already paid for once. And I did have some funds on hand, if we needed it.

Mom gave a long sigh. "Okay, then get going. The crowds get worse by the hour."

I tucked my little notebook and a pen into one back pocket, my phone in the other, moving the coin to the side cargo pocket of my shorts, which buttoned closed.

All of my notes for Rome so far (not many) were in the notebook. I'd write entries as we went to each place, while it was still fresh. Then I'd type all my notes up at once before turning them in the night before we flew out.

I didn't have much time, but a small piece of hope unfolded inside me. Maybe I really wouldn't fail.

"Be safe," Mom warned. "Learning is important, but your safety comes first, got it?"

I gave her my best smile. "I'll be with Vivi, Mom. We'll be fine."

An expression I didn't recognize crossed her face, almost like she couldn't quite make up her mind if she was happy or sad. "Okay. But remember, I want to see you here after lunch."

"You got it. Thanks, Mom!"

"Hey!" Dad looked up from his research.

I grinned, a real one. "Thanks, Mom. *And* Dad."

Two down, one to go. As tough as my parents were, I knew they'd be nothing compared to Vivi's dad. But when I arrived ready to plead our case, Vivi was already wrapping him up in a tight ball of string. There were definitely layers to this girl.

"Please, Papa? See, Lucas got permission. And Mr. and Mrs. Duran said they would be so grateful for any help."

Well, they hadn't, but they would have if they thought of it.

Mr. Bonacelli sighed deeply. "Since your parents agree, Lucas, I will give my permission as well. Just for today, Viviana. You can take evening shift tonight."

"Great, thank you, sir!" I said. "My parents will be so relieved to know I'll have an Italian guide as I do my research." I didn't have to fake my sincerity on that.

"Ready?" I asked Vivi.

She gave her dad a kiss and closed the door (cutting off his steely-eyed glare at me), leaving us alone in the hall. "Rome won't know what hit her."

CHAPTER FIVE
The Colosseum

One cool thing about Rome was how easy it was to get around. The Metro got people to all the big tourist places, even if you had to walk a few minutes to the nearest station or swap lines to get to your destination. Maybe Austin could try a monorail one of these days.

We got on at Barberini Station, grabbing two seats next to each other.

Vivi said, "We'll get lots of good stuff for your project *and* have a great time. We can do both, you know." She grinned up at me, and I suddenly felt much more hopeful.

Vivi and I swapped Metro lines at Termini Station, hopped onto the B line, and after a quick couple of minutes, we reached Colosseo Station. We followed a stream of tourists to the street, squinting at the brightness.

The Colosseum was just as large and crowded as it had been yesterday. The Arch of Constantine stood proudly in front of it, looking tiny in comparison, though it was no slouch of a monument itself.

"Get ready for some great photos!" Vivi cooed.

Two guys pranced around in red cloaks and fake shields

nearby, posing with some tourists. I jerked my thumb at them. "I'll pass on the actors. If I turned in shots of those guys, my art teacher would fail me for sure."

She laughed. "I think your friends back home might like you posing with a gladiator."

"Yeah, but these guys have plastic swords. Stores in America sells more realistic outfits on Halloween."

"America sounds very exciting," she said. "All those people, always on the go with new ideas and things to do and see!"

"Exciting? I guess, sometimes." I shrugged. "It's not like we live in New York City or something. But Austin's home, you know? That's what makes it so special. Rome is a lot more famous. I'd think it would be pretty exciting to live where ancient Romans cheered on gladiators."

"This place"—she gestured to the crowds—"is part of Rome, but it's not really a part of my life, if that makes sense."

I considered that. "Yeah, like I live in Texas, but I don't live on a cattle ranch. I don't even own a cowboy hat."

"Is that not illegal in Texas?" she teased. "I should like a picture of you in one when you get back. With cowboy boots!"

I snorted, lifting up my tennis-shoe-clad foot. "Believe it or not, lots of us don't own cowboy boots, either. But I'm sure I can get hold of a hat, if you insist."

She patted my arm. "Oh, I do."

Added to my mental list: GET COWBOY HAT.

But I didn't really want to think about Austin right now. I was here, and the sky was bright blue above us, even more vivid than a Texas spring sky. The scent of some sweet flower blew on the breeze. I took a deep breath.

Having a failing grade didn't seem *quite* so awful all of a sudden.

We paused at the triumphal arch—the Arch of Constantine—outside the Colosseum to take a selfie, which seemed to be obligatory. She crowed, "Today, I get to pretend to be a tourist!"

I pointed to the lengthy line already forming to go inside the Colosseum. "A real tourist would wait in lines just like this!"

"Lucky for us, we get special treatment." She did a little shimmy.

As we got in a line marked for special passes, I took a few pics of the outside, but they looked pretty standard. My art teacher, Ms. Deblasio, would not be happy with that. Lying down on the ground would give a cool angle . . . but that was too weird. People would stare. Or step on me.

There'd be more interesting options inside. I pocketed my phone, turning instead to Vivi. She was studying the crowd around us, lips pursed. "There are people from literally all over the world. It's so interesting."

I said, "When I'm stuck in line with my brothers, we make up stories about the people around us. Just silly stuff. It helps pass the time."

She grinned. "Oh, I see!" She nudged me. "See that man with the green backpack?"

I nodded. The guy had a beard and wrap-around shades, with

three-foot thick arm muscles. "Hollywood action star? Here to scope out the scene for his next movie."

She leaned closer to whisper. Her breath tickled my ear. "No, I think he's an undercover agent on a stakeout. When he gets the nod, he'll dive-roll out of line and handcuff the lady in the red coat right there. She's a spy from Russia, I think."

"What about that older lady with her?" I gestured to a gray-haired woman in a rose-print shawl, leaning on the arm of the red-coated woman posing in front of the Arch.

"Oh, she's the turncoat who's going to give the agent the secret signal."

The old woman picked her nose.

"I don't think that's the signal," I said.

We both giggled.

Then she smacked my arm. "Oh my goodness!"

"Hey!" I rubbed my arm. She was stronger than she looked.

"Sorry, but look! That guy back there in black leather?"

He was chewing gum and reading a brochure. "Yeah?"

"I think he's Steve Reddy, the lead singer in that band Silent Scream on tour in the city. Wow! I guess he's fitting in a quick jaunt to the Colosseum." Her voice trilled, and she bounced on the balls of her feet a few times.

I hadn't heard of them, but she seemed pretty jazzed. "So go ask him if you can get a picture with him, then!"

She shook her head. "That's not why we're here!"

"We're here to have fun, too, though, right?"

"I don't need to talk to him. I'm having fun already." She flashed a smile at me and I couldn't help but smile back.

The special speed-pass tickets definitely seemed like magic. In the time it took for our conversation, we'd whisked past the poor tourists in the regular line.

Vivi spoke in quick Italian for me at the head of the line. The guard winked and said something back.

"He said there's a special exhibit about local establishments that have been here for generations," she explained as we passed through the turnstiles. "Something a little bit special for your project."

Then she stopped and gazed upward. "Wow. Look at this place."

The ceiling of the breezeway soared high above us. The arches along the outside, barred with metal gates, glowed bright white in contrast to the dim interior of the building. I wrinkled my nose at the musty smell. The stone looked sooty at the top of the walls.

I hadn't noticed any of that last time. Pulling out my little notebook from my back pocket, I wrote down my observations. I wasn't sure if it was the right kind of stuff, but it was something.

"Come on," Vivi said, tugging at my arm. "Let's go higher! You can get some great shots from the top!"

As we headed up the stairs to the next level, tons of tourists shuffled along around us. She absentmindedly tucked her hand into the crook of my elbow. I didn't pull my arm back. The floor was rough in places. She could fall, you know. That was the only reason I kept my arm like that.

She paused at a display case, dropping my arm to point at the plaque inside the glass. "The oldest known image of the Colosseum is on a coin from 80 AD! That's pretty amazing!"

Her eyes glowed as she spoke. Her enthusiasm was kinda contagious.

"I'll write that down, thanks," I said. "I need lots of unique and little-known facts for my report."

"Then we'll read all of these displays!"

Not exactly my idea of a good time. But with Vivi, reading about history was a lot better.

Informational displays were set up inside the interior hallways, with small benches to rest. Ancient statues lounged in several locations. What *was* it with these ancient guys and their naked statues? They just begged to be mocked. I glanced at Vivi and kept walking. Today's photos would need to be a little higher class.

Kei would just have to miss out on that laugh.

Vivi asked, "Shall we go to the top and work our way down? History or no, it's a view you must include in your journal."

We started climbing again. She hummed under her breath like we weren't hiking practically straight vertical.

Note for my future journal entry on the Colosseum: there are many stairs here. Some of them are very, very steep. Some are worn down, very slick and smooth. Sometimes they're all of the above. At least I wore good tennis shoes.

When we finally reached the top level, Vivi threw her arms wide and laughed.

The wind blew her curly, dark hair from her face, leaving a clear shot of her profile, outlined by the deep blue Roman sky. It was a perfect composition—that's why I noticed. I wished I had the guts to ask if I could take her picture. For Ms. Deblasio. She'd love it.

I cleared my throat. "So, is it a cliché tourist trap?"

"Oh Lucas! It's actually amazing! I hadn't realized how much I'd love it! Thank you!"

I squirmed a bit, thinking of my initial plan to keep her from coming. I was glad I'd been foiled.

Vivi gave a long sigh and took a picture of the view herself. "No wonder tourists keep coming."

No wonder. Outside, it took very little imagination to see how things used to be. Even I could picture it. The oval of the arena behind us was surrounded by the rising tiers of stone, like the stands in a football stadium. Tourists lined the balconies today like gladiator fans might have then. I hoped they made cushions in the old days. The viewers' rears would be numb before the lion ate the first guy. I took the obligatory shot of the stadium seating.

Beyond the Colosseum, the ancient Roman Forum stood nearby—beautiful green fields littered with broken white columns and half-standing ancient Roman architecture. The sheer history of the area hovered over it like some powerful perfume.

I took a few snaps of the columns from here, zooming in close. They looked stark and jagged against the green fields.

"Like a bunch of broken bones," Vivi muttered.

She was exactly right. Maybe she wouldn't mind if I used that in my journal. I'd ask. It sounded like it could be poetry.

On our way back down the steps to the next level, my thighs quickly started burning. Man, I really needed to get back into shape.

"Let's see what's on this level inside," I said. An archway in the stands led back to the inside hallways. The interior seemed extra dark after the brilliance of the sky. I stepped out of the main thoroughfare to let my eyes adjust (and, okay, fine, to give my legs a chance to rest).

A strangely shaped person stood in the corner. *Wait.* That wasn't one person—it was two people, entwined with each other. And they were kissing.

Heat burst across my face. "Whoops, sorry!" *Awkward.* I spun to head in the opposite direction. Vivi must not have seen me turning in the dim light, and we collided like cartoon characters.

"Oof!" she said, landing on her backside.

I fell forward, tangled in her legs, and I yelped a high-pitched soprano note that could break glass. Never had I wanted a screaming toddler nearby as much as I did in that moment, so I could blame the shriek on anyone but me. No such luck, though, especially since my face was right in front of Vivi's.

Her eyes were very wide, and we stared at each other for a

long moment in shock. I'd probably knocked the breath out of her. I was definitely having a hard time catching mine.

She finally shook her head. "I'm so sorry, Lucas. That sounded like it hurt!"

"Nah, I'm fine," I said, struggling to stand up. "But I'm really sorry I ran into you!" Dude, I practically killed her. The embarrassment might kill *me*.

She sat up, rubbing her elbow. Her eyes narrowed as she looked past me to where the two-morphed-into-one stood. Awareness flooded her face, and she lifted one eyebrow.

Jeez. They were still at it. Not even our star-inducing fall had distracted them. Maybe they were newlyweds, taking their passion for Rome a little too far. I told her, "I, uh, didn't want to interrupt." My skin felt sunburned. "Can we go now?"

A smile quirked at the corners of her mouth. "Of course, come on, let's go back outside to see the amphitheater floor."

We exited the stairs at the second level and leaned on the low stone wall that separated this level from the lowest seating level.

Neither of us said a word for a long minute. What was I supposed to say? She was probably insulted I'd dragged her into that corner; she was probably embarrassed, no, *mortified;* she was probably—

Giggling. She was giggling.

Excuse me? I turned to her. "Are you really laughing right now?"

"You should have seen your face."

"No thanks." I tried not to hunch my shoulders and failed.

"It's odd you Americans get so flustered about kissing when your movies have so much of it. Did you at least get a good shot of them? You could add that to your WC photos." She nudged my shoulder with her own. She met my eyes, lips squeezed tight.

We both burst into laughter.

My armpits were sweating even though my laughter was real. The whole situation was *embarrassing*-funny, and that kind of humor worked best on TV. I'd seen people kissing before. It just took me by surprise here. I mean, I knew guys in our grade who'd had girlfriends, but it still seemed like something for later. Eighth grade wasn't high school yet.

Suddenly, later felt a lot sooner.

Shaking my head ruefully, I said, "Well, now that I've been totally humiliated, I guess it's time to get serious about my report."

"Good idea. You can see how new the wood floor is from here," she said, mercifully changing the topic back to the Colosseum.

She was right—and observant. I needed to start noticing stuff, too, if I was going to pass. *Look harder, Lucas.*

The wood floor covered part of the grounds so visitors could see where the fights actually took place, but it also revealed the tunnels underneath where contestants or even animals would wait for their turn in the arena. The wooden area looked like a small stage and reminded me a bit of the Globe Theatre in London, actually. But the tunnels beneath were roughly carved, with moss and dirt. It was dark in the sections covered by the boards.

"It had to have been terrifying," Vivi murmured, leaning her elbows on the stone wall.

"What?" I glanced over at her.

"To be a gladiator," she clarified. "To know you had to fight in front of this screaming crowd, all those people here to watch you die."

"Not exactly WWE, true."

"WW . . . E?" Her brow wrinkled.

"Wrestling. Like, fake movie-star-style wrestling." I tilted my head. "You know?"

She looked at me blankly.

My jaw dropped. "John Cena? Dwayne 'The Rock' Johnson? A.J. Styles? No? I'll show you sometime later and—"

Except we didn't really have a later. I'd almost forgotten. "Never mind. You, uh, made a good point about the gladiators."

Vivi pointed at the underground tunnels with an earnest glance at me. "Imagine it, Lucas! The screaming of the people above, the roars of the lion across the stadium. Coming for you." She shivered. "Makes our troubles seem pretty light. Though I'll never understand how anyone voted for the death of a fellow human being like it was a carnival."

I remembered Robby yesterday, going on and on about the gladiators, but I had been hot and tired and hungry. I hadn't even climbed to the top with my family. It hadn't seemed worth the effort.

But today, it was like the Colosseum was revealing itself to me through Vivi's eyes.

I felt very . . . small. The exposed passageways at the center of the structure looked almost like a strange flower unfolding. It had stood all this time.

I took a quick snap of it with my phone camera and caught a perfect shot, highlighting the moss-lined paths clear and crisp in the center of the photo.

The image wasn't anything I'd seen on tourist postcards or calendars. And it was unique. Just right for my assignment. And pretty cool, if I said so myself.

A flash of heat burned against the outside of my leg. I slapped my hand over my cargo pocket. Warmth radiated from within.

Vivi was saying, "And to think, the mood of the crowd could determine if you lived or died!"

The heat grew worse. "Ow!" I flipped open the pocket and dug out the coin, which was hot enough to sting my palm.

"What is it?" Vivi asked.

"Something's going on with the coin."

She said something, I think, but her voice faded. A bright light had me squinching my eyes closed. In the blackness, all I could hear was a roaring, like a crashing wave or . . . an angry lion.

Swampy heat stole over me, along with the powerful smell of many people standing in the heat for hours. I blinked, wiping sudden sweat from my brow.

When I opened my eyes, Vivi was gone. Thousands of people surrounded me. And for some reason, they were all wearing togas and tunics, looking amazingly like ancient Romans.

CHAPTER SIX

The First Trip

Gasping, I shook my head, but the vision in front of me remained. The sun wasn't as blinding now—above me, a huge canopy hung suspended over part of the stands from the top level, casting welcome shade over the thunderous crowds. Past the heads of the people in front of me—who all seemed to be men—was the Colosseum floor I'd just been staring at. But like the seats around me, the floor wasn't empty, either.

The crowd roared at that moment, and it was a physical blow to my chest. The noise landed with the same power as the gladiator's sword on his enemy.

Did I mention the gladiator yet?

Yeah. There was a gladiator. Two, actually. And they were fighting. And their swords sure didn't look fake.

Neither did the blood streaming down their bodies, glittering on their swords.

My throat was so dry I couldn't even squeak.

"Pretty impressive, isn't it?" a familiar voice said at my shoulder.

The palm reader stood next to me, smiling serenely as if she appeared in ancient Rome every day. Was this really happening?

She was wearing a toga, but it was still tie-dyed, which was even more surreal.

I gaped at her, probably looking like a fish that just flopped itself out of the fishbowl.

She patted my arm. "Give it a minute. We have all the time in the world." Then she cackled and leaned over to whisper, "You're lucky Romans like baths so much. Otherwise with this many people crammed in like sardines, in 100 AD, for hours in the heat? No thank you." She waved a hand in front of her nose in the universal symbol for *stinky*.

Was she insane?

Was I?

It certainly felt real. The press of the bodies on either side of me was firm. When I closed my eyes and took in a deep breath, the earthy smell of sweat, blood, and sand filled my nose. Daylight glowed against my closed lids, as if denying me any escape.

I swallowed hard and managed to croak, "We've . . . traveled back in time?"

She shouted with the crowd as the less bloody man landed another blow on his opponent. "Looks like it, doesn't it? The coin is definitely one of a kind."

Virtual reality, maybe? I touched my face, my hands, my ears . . . wouldn't I feel goggles?

She clucked her tongue. "You should be taking notes. You write out a live-action scene like this for your journal, and your history teacher's going to love you."

Electricity shot down my spine. "*That's* what this is about?"

She winked. "Well. Mother Rome has many reasons for many things. Let's just say your need for information dovetails nicely with her own plans to answer your wish."

"Wish?" I sounded like an idiot, but I couldn't help it. My brain was turning inside out.

"On the fountain, yes. Oh my, you look a little green. The first trip never lasts long, don't worry." She patted my shoulder.

The *first* trip? My knees gave out, and I plunked down on my concrete seat—no cushion—and got an accidental elbow jab in the head from my neighbor's enthusiastic clapping.

That sure felt real.

I looked around me. Real or not, the excitement in the air crackled like something I could touch. The men around us started screaming again, veins cording their necks. There was a blood-thirstiness that sent an icy shock of fear through me. This was a mob. Mobs were dangerous.

"Okay, I think I've got a good idea, thanks. Can we go now?" I turned to the palm reader.

But she wasn't there.

More breath wheezed out—I was going to completely collapse right here in ancient Rome (*ancient Rome?!*), and my family would never know what happened to me.

A cloying need to escape lit my feet on fire. "Excuse me," I said trying to push past the enthusiastic toga-wearing man to my right. The stone stands were arranged in five levels, and I was on the second, with only the senators below in their special togas. If I remembered correctly, I could slip out through the arch to our right and then find the stairs. *And then what, Lucas?* It wasn't like I could hop on a plane to the future.

"Get him!" shouted my neighbor at the men below. He beat on his chest and screamed. I stopped trying to push past him. Mental note: Don't make him mad.

"We love you, Flamma!" a woman behind us shouted. All the ladies were in the next level up, but they were just as into the games as the men. Which was saying something. This was like a Texas versus Oklahoma football game on steroids.

"Oh, he's got him! *Habet!* He's got the Gaul!" someone nearby shouted. I didn't want to look, but I couldn't stop myself. Goosebumps popped along my arms.

The tallest gladiator, with about a thousand pounds of muscle, stood over the shorter one, grimy with blood and sand sticking to him from the floor. *Huh.* They used sand down there. I guess to soak up the blood, jeez.

The man on the ground dropped his shield and sword and raised his hand with a finger up. The winner turned to face the crowds and opened his arms wide, showboating like a WWE champion.

The crowd went nuts. I clamped my hands over my ears, but I could still hear them shouting:

"Kill him! Kill him!" I suddenly realized I could understand everyone just fine in . . . Latin, I think? More magic.

Plenty others were shouting, "Let him go!" with lowered thumbs.

The man next to me was a Death voter, waving his arms madly—I had to duck a few times—and giving a thumbs up. He drew his hand across his throat in a cartoony signal that worked well to translate in case I had any doubts.

Holy cow. I didn't want to see anyone die today.

The words burst from me in a shriek: "*No!* Please, have mercy! Let him go!

The man next to me scoffed at me, "Foolish boy."

"You can see me?" I blurted but then quickly added, "He's just a man, like you and me!"

"A criminal!" he spat.

"Maybe—but still a human being!" An idea struck me. I lifted my palms, trying to look like I knew what I was talking about. "And if he doesn't die, he can fight again! Such potential!"

The man pondered this, nodding slowly. Then he laughed, changed his thumb from up to down, and said, "I feel generous today."

The gladiator backed away slowly from his opponent, and the emperor stood and said something I couldn't hear. But it looked like the losing gladiator was going to live. Today, at least.

I didn't realize how scary it would be, and I wasn't even the one in the ring. It was one thing to see the old stone walls, but another to see them filled with screaming people—people ready to watch two men fight to the death. That was nuts. This was . . .

Real.

Vivi's voice came to me, sounding far away and echoey, but I couldn't quite make out her words.

The roaring got louder, but it was different, more like the ocean or a storm. Heat grew along the side of my leg again. I dug out the coin, and the temperature stung my palm. I didn't let go, though.

The sun got unbearably bright, and I threw one arm over my eyes. When I opened them, Vivi was saying, "What is it?"

I blinked. "What?"

"You said something was going on with the coin. It seemed to flash, but I think it just reflected the sun."

Frantically, I looked around, but the stands were full of tourists, not ancient Romans. The sun was warm, but there was no canvas canopy overhead, no screams, no men fighting below.

My knees gave out again. "I, uh, thought I, uh . . ."

How on earth could I explain this? It sounded crazy. Maybe it was.

I hesitated. Lying wouldn't be too hard . . . but the thought of keeping something so big to myself made me feel like exploding. I couldn't help but spill it. "Hear me out. Either your description of history was super incredible, or this coin helped me visit the past. And talk to someone there."

Her eyebrows rose. "The coin did what, did you say?" She looked like she might be wondering if I was getting sunstroke.

What was I thinking? I shook my head. Too much. "Nothing, forget it. I must have . . . hallucinated."

"You saw the gladiators?" She tilted her head to one side. "Imagined them? Or . . . *saw* them?"

I gave a weak chuckle. Better to just rip off the bandage now.

"I know how it sounds. But I *saw* them. One man even spoke to me—I told him not to vote to kill the loser. It was . . . insane. Scary, like I'd slid into some movie or video game." I let out a long breath. "I'd never be able to make all that up myself."

Her eyes narrowed, then widened. She took a half step back.

Oh no. She wasn't buying it. And why would she? I sounded like an idiot. Totally nuts. I lifted one shoulder, trying to play it off. "Nah, never mind. It was probably just like a daydream or something. From the heat. And too many movies."

Her smile grew huge. "Well, *I* think it sounds like a miracle. Don't you agree?"

My mouth fell open. "You don't think I'm crazy?"

"Listen, if you are, I'd like to be, too!" She gasped and said, "Ooh, the woman who gave us the tickets today—she gave you this coin, no?"

"She did." Was Vivi just patting me on the head to make me feel better? Maybe, but I'd take it over laughing at me.

"Do you think it'll happen again?" She studied me, her face giving nothing away.

"God, I hope not," I muttered, but Vivi was already moving, brow drawn in deep thought.

Inside the curved hallway in one of the middle levels—I'd lost track—she asked me a thousand questions about the trip, and I did my best to answer. Finally, I waved for mercy and collapsed on a bench near a temporary display of black-and-white photographs of the history of the area.

An occasional breeze wafted through from the outside, where

other big monuments and buildings waited. My brain spun a million miles a minute, but no matter what just happened, I still had to finish my journal. I only had today, Saturday, Sunday, and maybe a few hours on Monday before we flew out. No time to sit here in shock.

"You should write it down now," Vivi said. "Even if it was the world's most vivid daydream, it will be great for your school journal. You'll forget otherwise."

I didn't want to. I wanted to run to the next place, not do the hard work of wrestling words. Or run screaming back to my parents and beg them to take me home to Texas right now.

Get it together, Lucas.

"Good idea. It'll take me a few minutes, though. I write kinda slow." Heat burned my neck. I'd already blurted that I was failing school, but there was no need to drive it home. If she saw my scrawl that passed for handwriting . . .

"I've got plenty of time—I'll just look around while you work."

My notebook was awfully plain and mostly empty. I sat on the bench. Reading through my notes from earlier, plus a discarded brochure on the ground, I finally wrote a full entry.

Dear Ms. Morris, Ms. Deblasio, and Mr. Franklin,

I went to the Colosseum twice, but luckily, I didn't have to fight a lion either time. Did you know that gladiators really were forced to fight animals and each other for entertainment there? It was loud and crazy during fights.

Smelly, too. If you were a gladiator and got a thumbs up, too bad for you—you weren't leaving there alive. You'd think a thumbs up would be a good thing, but no. It is pretty amazing to think about how just one moment can change everything for someone. It had to be really scary for those gladiators, but most didn't have a choice, which is awful.

Anyway, the Colosseum is really big and holds 50,000 people! That's a lot of togas. And it took Rome just eight years to build it. The legend is that as long as this building stands, so will Rome. I don't think there's anything to worry about. An earthquake in 1349 did take down one part of the wall, but the rest is hanging on just fine.

Standing inside that building, I realized how easy it was to forget that history was full of people just like you and me. Those people in our books . . . they were someone's family, someone's friend. It really puts a lot into perspective. Next time I read a history book, I'll remember that the people in the stories were just like me.

Sincerely,

Lucas

I didn't believe that last line. The people who made history weren't like me—they were way smarter—but it sounded good for my report. Maybe my teachers would be more likely to give me an A.

Now what, though? One thing for sure—I never would have been able to write an entry that good without the kick in the rear from whatever just happened. Instead of fearing it would happen again, maybe I should start hoping for it. It might be the only way I'd pass.

Vivi and I wandered to the photographs of the historical area. "Ooh, I know this place!" she said, pointing to one of the photos. "This restaurant is near the Metro, a few blocks away. It looks the same, even though this is such an old photo!"

The image was black and white, faded around the edges, curling at the corners. Booths lined each side of the room, with round bistro tables in the middle. Customers wearing old-timey clothes sat drinking tiny cups of cappuccino. Heaping plates of spaghetti were on the far table. A waitress wearing an apron with *Trattoria Russo* scrolled across the front smiled at the young family in the booth, holding a platter full of fresh bread.

The woman looked familiar. I examined the image closer. Her hair was short and spiky—definitely at odds with the styles of whatever time this was. I narrowed my eyes, examining that ever-so-slightly-blurry face . . . and caught the three hearts tattooed along her arm.

"No way!" The words exploded from me.

"What is it? Lucas, are you okay?" Vivi put her hand on my arm, but I barely felt it.

"That's her! That's the lady who gave me the coin. The palm reader."

Her brows lifted. "The waitress there? In this . . . very old photograph?"

Chills raced over my scalp and slapped me on the face on

their way down to my toes. The woman looked the same. She hadn't changed at all. "That's impossible."

"Or that's . . . a miracle," Vivi corrected. Her eyes were beginning to do that sparkling thing again.

The photograph looked super old, like it was from 60 or 70 years ago, or more. The palm reader looked elderly in that photo, so she sure shouldn't be handing out coins to young Americans in Italy today, looking exactly the same.

Was it a miracle? Or some kind of practical joke? A con job taken to an extreme? But how could she have gotten this picture behind the official display glass at a national monument like the Colosseum?

Maybe I really did just travel in time. My heart gave a hard squeeze in my chest.

I took a picture of the picture. "I've got to get to that place," I blurted.

Vivi nodded. "It's not far from our shop. I can take you there."

The energy coursing through me threatened to bubble into a freaked-out scream if we didn't get moving. My legs trembled. "Can we go now? They must know something about her. It sounds nuts, I know, but you've got to believe me—"

"I do." She cut me off with a smile. "You told me already that this palm reader knew about me somehow, too. This woman in the picture could be her mother, or her grandmother, but maybe there's true magic in the world and we're a part of it. How wonderful would that be?"

She had a point, actually, but . . . "I just need to pass eighth grade." I scrubbed a hand over my face.

"Wait, I thought you were trying to pass a project?"

Whoops. I hadn't meant to tell her about my maybe soon-to-be complete failure. Too late now. Tingling heat swept along my neck and across my face. "Well, the project is really important, so if I fail it, I'll fail my grade. For the year."

Her dark eyes swam with sympathy. "Oh Lucas! No wonder you've been so upset! Then let's go find this woman so we can get back to our tour for the day."

Maybe the restaurant would offer a clue. Or some history I could add to the report. At the very least, we could eat lunch while we were there, and I could write about it for my English teacher if I described the food in pretty words. I had to fit a poem into my project somehow anyway.

I glanced at Vivi in the late-morning sun. It was too bad we hadn't taken this day together sooner. It would have made my time in Rome a lot better.

CHAPTER SEVEN

Trying Something New

The restaurant would have been easy to miss, tucked between a dress shop and a market, but Vivi led me straight there. The red lettering *Trattoria Russo* curlicued its way across the big glass window, fading to a dark bubblegum pink on the bottom edges where the afternoon sunlight slipped under its awning.

I took a quick snapshot for my records and jotted down the name. I couldn't forget to take notes—that was kinda the whole point of today, time travel or no time travel. If I actually failed eighth grade, seeing a mob cheering for some dude's death wouldn't be the scariest thing I'd see this week. My mom's furious-yet-disappointed expression would take first place.

As soon as we entered, the scent of tomato sauce, garlic, and fresh-baked bread surrounded us. The rich smells were as good as my favorite barbeque spot back home, just different.

My stomach rumbled, super loud, and I glanced at Vivi sheepishly.

She giggled. "I'm hungry, too. Shall we eat while we are here?"

Vivi spoke so formally sometimes. It made me smile. "We shall!"

She rolled her eyes and slid into a booth, and I sat across from her. We appeared to be the first customers of the day. Striped black-and-white wallpaper set off red leather booth chairs and the red tablecloths. It looked sharp, not at all dated, despite still having the same décor as in the old photograph.

"They just opened for the day," Vivi explained while she browsed the menu. "Oh, it says here that they've been around for generations."

"What about plain ol' spaghetti and tomato sauce?" I asked, thinking back to that picture of the palm-reader-turned-waitress with the giant platter of noodles.

"Sometimes simple is best." She set the menu aside with a smile.

An elderly woman approached our table, wearing the exact apron from the old photo, but this wasn't the tattooed coin lady. This woman had black hair streaked with gray, pulled back in a bun. She looked rounder and softer, too, like someone's grandma who just finished baking cookies.

"*Bon giorno!*" she spoke with warmth. A flurry of Italian followed between her and Vivi, and introductions seemed to be exchanged.

"Oh, forgive me!" Vivi broke the conversation, looking at

me. "This is Lucas. He's looking for someone who once worked here. Lucas, this is Signora Russo, one of the owners."

I swallowed hard. "The lady we're looking for has short spiky hair? Older?"

The woman laughed. "Older, like my age, you'd say?"

My foot felt wedged into my mouth. I had no idea how to guess old people's ages. "Maybe?" I gave a weak smile and turned to Vivi for help.

"Older," Vivi said firmly.

I added, "With heart tattoos running down one arm."

The smile slipped off the woman's face. "Heart tattoos?" She paused, her eyes narrowing. Her next words came out slowly, but with growing certainty. "Did she give you . . . a coin?"

Electricity zipped through me, and I sat up straighter in my seat. "Yes. Yes! Have you seen her?"

She gave an understanding smile that made my eyes sting for some reason. "Just *un momento*. You must be hungry. Lunch is on the house. We have a special you'll love."

"Oh, but—" I began, but she'd already hurried into the kitchen.

"That was weird, wasn't it?" I asked Vivi. I twisted and untwisted my napkin, keeping an eye on the doorway to the kitchen.

"She definitely knew something." Her wrinkled brow cleared. "Maybe you'll get your answer!"

A heartbeat later, Signora Russo slid a plate onto the table, with two greenish-brown things. What was that?

Vivi broke into a broad grin. "Oh yum! *Carciofi alla giudìa*!"

"Car what?" I asked.

She laughed along with Signora Russo, who explained, "Fried artichokes. It's a very popular dish in Rome. Have you not tried it yet?"

I cleared my throat, studying the plate with growing concern. "Must have missed this one."

The woman tut-tutted. "Then you have missed one of the most Roman dishes there is! These are fresh artichokes, deep-fried twice in olive oil."

The fried artichokes looked like some kind of weird fried flower or a weed. Crisped and brown around the edges, with hints of green and almost yellow inside the centers. Not exactly top dining, in my book.

Vivi picked up an artichoke by the thin stem, plucked off one of the petals—leaves?—and popped it into her mouth with a crunch. *Really?* "Mmm! Perfect!"

Signora Russo bowed slightly. "We try our humble best."

Vivi pulled off another petal and held it out to me. "Come on, now, Lucas! You can write about it in your journal!"

I almost grimaced, but then caught myself and forced a smile. No need to offend Signora Russo. And it would make Vivi happy. And it could definitely work for a poem. Mr. Franklin once described a delicious steak in a poem for a class example, the only time poetry had ever seemed interesting. I scribbled a few lines in my notebook and then closed it quick:

Here I am in Rome,
Eating a weed from the side of the road
Fried up to look fancy.
Like me when I had to wear a tux
To my aunt's wedding.

Reaching forward, I gingerly took the little vegetable piece from her hand. It was still warm. But it was also greenish and oily.

If Kei were here, he'd say *I dare you, dude!* He'd get a kick out of me eating something that looked like a deep-fried corsage gone wrong.

Fine. Here went nothing.

I closed my eyes and tossed it in my mouth. The crispy piece of artichoke tasted like . . . chips. But maybe even better? My eyes popped open. "It's good!"

Vivi shook a finger at me. "Next time, believe me when I tell you something."

But there won't be a next time. Which was a bit of a bummer, I realized. But I didn't say anything.

I pushed the thought of leaving aside, and we demolished the fried artichokes—apparently anything tastes good when deep-fried twice in olive oil and soon Signora Russo was back with two round plates, both heaped with spaghetti.

Thank goodness, a food I knew how to eat. The tangy tomato sauce and perfectly cooked pasta made my mouth water and sidelined the unbelievable morning. This was solid. Real.

"Finish lunch before we talk," Signora Russo said. "I have a few things to take care of first." She scurried away. Vivi and

I shrugged at each other and dug in. There wasn't much time for chatter—the smell of the garlicky goodness had us both attacking our plates.

Mental note to self: if I ever take a girl on a date—this definitely wasn't a date—do not order spaghetti. I got sauce on my chin, on my nose, and on my shirt. I was talented that way. Luckily, I was fast with a napkin. Helping out my brothers gave me lots of practice.

When our plates were all but licked clean, Signora Russo pulled up a chair to the edge of our booth rather than sliding in next to me or Vivi. With just the three of us in the room, the moment felt hushed . . . magical.

The signora pulled out a photo book. "First, you should know I've been expecting you."

She must have seen the suspicion on my face because she smiled. "Oh, not you, exactly. But someone with a coin. The woman you asked about has been here recently, the first time in many years. And she left me a gift to give to someone else. I believe it must be you." She slid two tickets across the table to me.

Examining them, I said, "These are the same kind of skip-the-line tickets that don't really exist, but they're for the Sistine Chapel." I looked closer. "One person and a guest, per ticket. For today."

Vivi gasped, hands flying to her cheeks. "And the second ticket is for me? But why give us two if we can each bring a guest?"

The signora shrugged. "You don't need a guest to use each

ticket. But before you go, I brought some pictures to share. It felt appropriate, if you are willing to stay a bit longer."

"Of course," I said. Vivi nodded. Here was an adult confirming that the magical lady was real.

This was all *real*.

Signora Russo creaked the cover open and pointed. "That is me and my sister, when we were about your age. Each photo in this book shows people who are part of my family. Let me tell you a story."

She spoke slowly. "I was not born in Rome. Some say that Romans are Roman first, Italian second. I felt this way, that I might not ever fit in. I came from the south, and my family was much poorer than many I met in Rome. But the city here—ah, there was so much to do and see and learn!"

Vivi was nodding along. I felt almost afraid to move.

"But I also felt terribly alone." The shop owner met my eyes. "It is hard to be away from home, is it not?"

I gulped, unable to look away. "It is."

Vivi patted my hand, warm and comforting. I managed a smile, and when she moved her hand away, turning her full attention back to the signora, it felt like a spotlight leaving me.

Signora Russo said, "Here in Rome, I felt different from everyone around me. Oh, I pretended to be like them, but city life did not come easily to me. I struggled every day, surrounded by confident strangers, embarrassed by my many failures." She licked her lips. "Home felt much safer. It wasn't perfect, but I knew how to get by there."

My throat was too tight to speak, but I nodded. I felt every word deep inside.

Vivi gave a deep sigh, leaning forward on her elbows.

The signora continued, "So I was just twenty years old, alone in the big city of Rome, when I met a young man whose family owned a trattoria. He invited me to join him for dinner, and I met his family. And they all hugged me, welcomed me. He showed me the city, took me all around, and before I knew it, he had asked me to marry him."

Vivi sighed. "How romantic!"

"I told him no." The signora clasped her hands together on the table.

"What?" Vivi sat bolt upright. "But—but you said he showed you the city! Welcomed you within his family!"

I didn't know beans about romance, but I thought I understood. Feeling down on yourself was no joke.

Signora Russo nodded like she could hear me. "And all I could think of was that eventually he'd see what I already felt: that I didn't belong here. I'd be leaving my home behind to stay where I felt foolish so often."

Foolish. Yeah, I got that, too. Last year, my school counselor told me I acted goofy and made people laugh to keep them from laughing at me first. I'd been sent to her office for not "trying my best." As mad as it had made me then, maybe she'd had a point.

But here Signora Russo was, today, in Rome. So . . . what changed for her?

"Did you?" I had to ask. "Go home?"

She turned the album, showing a photo of her with a group of people who looked a lot like her. "I did. I wasn't going to ever return to Rome, but before I left the city, a woman with wild hair and heart tattoos gave me a special coin and told me to wish on the Trevi Fountain."

"What kind of coin?" I interrupted, pulse pounding like a jackhammer in my chest.

"Oh, I think you know." Her smile wasn't sly like the coin lady's so often was. It was gentle and understanding, matched by a sympathy in her eyes that made me trust her.

I pulled the coin out of my pocket. "Like this?"

Her fingers trembled as she reached toward it, but then she pulled back her hand before touching it. "That one, or one just like it. Yes. She told me I'd come back one day and find my fate. That I would be happier for it . . . so I threw the coin. And you know what they say about wishing on that fountain, don't you?"

I nodded. "You'll return to Rome. I can't even count the number of times my mom's told us the story of how she wished on the fountain when she was a girl so she'd come back."

I curled my fingers around the thick coin and shoved it in my back pocket. I didn't want to be here, didn't want to come back. Right?

Signora Russo nodded. "I threw a coin, one like yours, and I did return to Rome. I also found love here, and married. But the coin did something else for me. Something beyond the possible."

She gave me a long, measured look, as if waiting for me to fill in the blank.

With my hands clasping the edge of the table, I asked, "Did you ever . . . see something . . . from the past?"

Relief spread across her face, followed by a touch of fear and pity. "I did. And while I'd never been so afraid, it taught me to trust myself in ways I never had before. Look here."

Vivi let out a long, slow breath. "It really did happen, then." Her words were barely audible.

The signora pulled out another photo, one of a young bride and a happy groom. "When I returned, I told my beloved yes. Fortunately, he had been waiting. And this has been my home ever since, and my children's, and their children's. But I wouldn't have believed in myself if the tattooed woman hadn't given me the little push." She met my eyes. "If history hadn't set me free to change my own future."

A shudder ran through me as I felt my world tilt on its axis. The palm reader really was Magical with a capital M. I had really traveled through time.

"What did you see?" the signora asked gently.

Vivi answered, her face aglow. "Lucas saw gladiators!"

She believed me. Tense muscles in my shoulders suddenly relaxed. Thank goodness she didn't think I was crazy. Judging from the new determination in Vivi's eyes, she was all in now.

And I guess I was, too.

Signora Russo winked at me. "My! I bet that was fascinating! I won't go into details about my own trip, lest my story somehow impacts yours, but let me just say . . . it was eye-opening. I'd encourage you to limit who you tell, too. Few will understand or believe what you already know is true."

Vivi whispered, "But you think she is a force for good? This woman?"

"I do."

I ran both hands through my hair, clutching the sides of my head for a second. "I want to believe it, too. I mean, how amazing is all this? She could be some kind of magician or witch—who knows? But it's . . . just . . . wow."

Vivi slapped her hands on the table. "Maybe she's a guardian angel to make sure you pass! How better to learn history than to *experience* it?"

That wasn't the vibe I got from her—more like she wanted to meddle in my personal life—but I didn't argue. "She was there, actually, back then in ancient Rome. When I got there. She said . . ." I couldn't even think about it: she'd called it my *first* trip.

I shook my head, gathering the Sistine Chapel tickets in my hand. "She gave me the coin—and now this second set of tickets—but I just need to make an A on my report about Rome. That doesn't seem like enough reason to send a kid through time. I mean, I'm grateful and all, but it seems like overkill, you know?"

Signora Russo shrugged in a way that seemed very Italian to me, with that what-will-be-will-be attitude. "I imagine she has another lesson for you to learn."

I slumped in my seat. "I'm not interested in another lesson. This one's hard enough."

Learning didn't come easy to me. My parents treated me and my brothers like we were their college students. I didn't understand half of what they talked about when they got on a roll at a tour site. They weren't bad parents at all . . . we just didn't have much in common.

My brothers were super smart like my parents, but they at least still saw me as someone to look up to, someone who could teach them stuff.

Not many people did.

Signora Russo interrupted my thoughts. "Just know, if she gave you a coin, there's a reason. The sooner you learn why, the sooner everything will fall into place. Maybe she's a fairy godmother, I don't know. But I'm thankful for her every day." She patted my shoulder and said, "Good luck with your report."

Well. We had new information but no answers. And a new place to go, apparently.

CHAPTER EIGHT

Extra Company

Signora Russo had needed to trust herself first in order to accept Rome as her home, but Rome wasn't my new home, and I didn't want it to be. Yet with magic involved, there had to be more to this than a great grade.

We offered our thanks and said goodbye. As we joined the crowds in the street, Vivi said, "We've got to follow the destinations this magic lady has laid out. She has some sort of plan. I hope I get to meet her!"

"But I still don't get her game. I've already been to the Sistine Chapel!"

Wagging a finger at me, she said, "The same way you'd been to the Colosseum? Did you really pay attention?"

"I—" *No.* My mouth closed with a snap, and I lifted my hands in surrender.

She gave me an arched smile. "That's what I thought. Let's go see Rome! Have an adventure! And get you out of eighth grade!" She laughed. "It's time to go check in with our parents, but then I'll hopefully have more time to go with you. I want to be there in case your coin gives you another little blast from the past."

"Maybe we'll even see her there," I mused.

Vivi nodded. "Definitely possible. Let's stop by the shop and then keep going."

On our way to the B&B, weaving through crowded sidewalks, Vivi put her hand on my arm. I had a sudden urge to flex my bicep for some reason, but she'd probably be able to tell I was trying. Besides, that was totally dumb.

She said, "Since you're learning lots about Rome, it's only fair I learn about Texas, I think. Tell me more about your home."

I blinked. "Really? After all that, you want to talk about *Texas?*"

She nodded emphatically. "I want to learn all about America, and Texas is part of that. And I've got an eyewitness right here with me."

"Oookay. Well, Texas is really big. It's bigger than a lot of the countries over here, even. I live in Austin, which is almost in the middle of the state."

"What's your city like?"

I paused, searching for words. How weird that I didn't even know how to describe my quirky-but-cool city, except that I loved it. "Well, its unofficial motto is 'Keep Austin Weird' if that tells you anything."

She laughed, and I warmed to my topic, my voice growing more animated. "Austin has great food, lots of Tex-Mex and barbeque. There's a few big parks where people go running or hang out at by the lake. Oh, and Austin has a big music scene!"

I turned to walk backwards for a few steps to get a good look at her face for this part. "Lots of live music, street buskers, that sort of thing."

That last line really seemed to grab her. She clapped her hands. "Oh, I love music! We have some excellent artists here, but I'd love to hear yours, too."

I wanted to tell her she should come visit sometime, but that would never happen. Besides the cost, why would she fly all that way just to see *me*?

"I think you'd like Texas," I said instead, falling back to pace at her side.

"Oh, I'm sure I would! You don't live on a cattle ranch, but surely there's still *some* cowboys there in Texas? With cowboy boots and hats and horses?" She bounced on tiptoes.

"Well, sometimes," I hedged, hating to disappoint her. "In the big cities, lots of people don't wear boots or hats, but plenty do. And if you live out in the country, you're way more likely to have a horse. I don't ride horses."

"And you already said you don't have a cowboy hat." Her smile quirked. "Maybe we should get you one here."

I scoffed. "If I show up at school in Texas with an *Italian* cowboy hat, I can promise you I'd never hear the end of it."

"Your friends would tease you, I bet. Especially Kei. Maybe I'll meet him one day," Vivi said, glancing at me hesitantly.

Between me and Kei, he was better at talking to girls. He'd even gone out with a couple. Would Vivi like hanging out with Kei more than me? A prickly feeling swirled inside me at the thought, but I nodded. "That'd be cool."

She smiled, and I was glad I'd said that. Pushing away the uncomfortable idea of worlds colliding one day, I asked, "Do you plan on traveling a lot one day, then? What, Rome not beautiful enough for you?" I waved my hand at the classic beautiful buildings all around us.

"I can't wait to travel, but if my father has his way, I'll never leave Rome. That's not what he wants for me." She scowled. I think it was the first time I'd seen her frown.

I wasn't quite sure what to do with a non-bubbly Vivi. But I was intrigued. "What does he want for you, then?"

Vivi pursed her lips. "My father wants me to go to university somewhere in Italy one day like my brothers. Staying in Rome would be even better. And in his dreams, we all work in the B&B when we grow up. It's been in our family for generations. My mom died when I was little, so I think it means even more to him that we all stay." Her words were matter-of-fact.

I didn't know what to say. "Oh, I'm sorry."

She shrugged. "It was a long time ago. It just means all the boys in my family want to keep me locked in a safe when I'm not at work or at school."

"That stinks. My parents don't trust me to make my own decisions, either." It didn't seem polite to tell her I'd begged to stay behind with Kei, but they'd overruled me and dragged me along on this trip. She might think I regretted meeting her, which I definitely did not.

"It's definitely frustrating sometimes." She sighed and looked down.

Dang, I'd bummed her out. So I nudged her shoulder. "I bet your dad just wants to keep you safe. Though you can clearly take care of yourself. I watched you with him—you had him around your finger!" I wiggled my pinky at her and grinned.

She slapped at my hand and laughed, finally. Whew. But then her smile turned down in concern. "You must really miss home after all these months away. I hope I haven't upset you, asking about it."

Her words caught me by surprise, and I hurried to clarify. "No! I mean, yeah, I miss it, but I don't mind talking about it." I blinked rapidly. It was true. Huh. Thinking about home didn't sting like it used to. What did that mean? Was it bad?

"And you must miss your friends, too." She studied me like she did everything. I wondered what she noticed. I straightened my shoulders.

"I do, but honestly? I'm not sure anyone at home has even noticed I'm gone." The words popped out but I didn't regret them. She'd been honest with me. She deserved the same. And she'd never make fun of someone's feelings, I could just tell.

"I doubt that! I bet when you get home in just a few days, you'll see that for yourself." Her tone was sympathetic, and her eyes were dark as they held mine.

Home seemed very far away right now. Vivi suddenly seemed way more real than Kei, more real than anyone back in Austin. It was kinda . . . scary, in a way, how hard it was to remember the details of home right this moment, while walking with cobblestones under my feet. Being here sort of felt like time traveling: it was vivid and real and full of history, but I didn't really *belong* here.

Then she shook her head and gave her cheery smile. Wow, her eyes could really sparkle. I always thought books made that stuff up. "And even if I never get to travel myself, at least I have interesting friends from all over the world." She nudged my shoulder this time, and the surreal, scary feeling disappeared.

When we arrived at the B&B, I left Vivi downstairs to go check in with my parents. No doubt they'd give me the afternoon with her. They'd want me to pass my class, no matter what. Nothing mattered more to them than learning and good grades. And luckily, I wasn't frustrated at having her keep me company anymore.

"Hey, Mom and Dad! Vivi offered to take me around a few more places this afternoon. Can I go?"

Dad glanced up from his computer and sort of grunted. Mom looked at me like she was starving and I'd just walked in holding a giant pizza.

"Lucas! Thank goodness! Listen. Your brothers are going stir-crazy. They're driving me bonkers. Take them with you!"

At just that moment, Robby's voice came from our bedroom. "Stop TOUCHING me, Trevor!"

"Mom, are you kidding?" I said, crossing my arms. "How can I pass my class if I'm babysitting?"

And then there was the thought of taking my loud brothers into the quiet sanctuary of the Sistine Chapel. I didn't remember much from our first time there, but I definitely remembered all the *shhs*. What if they embarrassed Vivi? Or embarrassed me in front of Vivi?

Trevor's squeal pierced the air, and Mom and I both winced. "Please?" she begged. "You can go with Vivi if you take your brothers!" Her voice grew loud. "Just get them out of the apartment!"

My brothers came running out of their room. "What? Yeah! Take us!"

I groaned, and Robby's eyes lit with challenge. "I could tell you about all the monuments."

"We're starting at the Sistine Chapel," I sighed. "You'll have to be quiet. You'll be bored."

"I could spend hours there and still have more to see," Robby argued. "Anyone could."

"Pleeease?" Trevor, at six, could beg like nobody's business. It usually worked, too. The little booger.

"Lucas, how can you say no?" Dad said, charmed as always. "Look at their faces!"

"I'm looking at them." I'd seen those faces covered in dirt, snot, and vomit. Sometimes all at once.

"We didn't get to go anywhere all morning," Robby said, "while you ran around all over the place. It's not fair."

The photographs from the café flickered through my mind. All those photos of Signora Russo with her sisters . . . I had almost none with my brothers. Which, now that I thought about it, was pretty sad. And I did have tickets that allowed a guest per ticket. Almost like the palm reader had known this would happen.

Goosebumps crawled along my skin. What *didn't* she know?

I nodded, sure now that the palm reader wanted the boys to come. "Can you stick with us and do everything we say?" I asked them.

"I can!" Trevor cried out, standing tall.

Robby said suspiciously, "Like what?"

That was my boy. He was smart in more ways than one. "You can't just run off, okay? You've got to hold one of our hands the whole time, and if we say we're done, we're done." And hopefully he wouldn't notice anything if I jumped back in time. Vivi had only known because I told her.

Robby folded his arms. "Deal, 'cept I'm not holding anyone's hand."

I considered, then offered a fist bump. "Only when crossing the street, then."

He rolled his eyes but bumped my fist in agreement. "Cars don't stop much for people here."

The kid had good observation skills, that's for sure. "Let's go," I said to the boys, and then to my parents, I offered, "Happy writing."

Mom gave her usual safety rundown, which included a thousand and one concerns. She had to be really stressed to let me take the boys out without her. Before we left, she told me, "I owe you one."

Trevor chose that moment to pinch Robby, who popped him on the head.

"Yeah you do," I said.

But even as we clamored down the stairs, the boys' focus turned from torturing each other to the upcoming afternoon. You could see it happen, a lightening of their moods. Maybe we'd survive after all.

As we swung around the corner to the shop, I called out, "Well, Vivi, you've got all three Duran brothers with you the rest of today. I hope that's okay with you!"

Vivi was behind the counter, cleaning, dark eyebrows drawn in a very un-Vivi-like scowl.

My pace slowed, my brothers hesitating at my heels. Maybe our plans were over before they started. Which meant my high school life might as well be over, too. I needed her help. "What's up? Can you still go?"

She wiped down the counter with excessive force. "Yes, I can go. After I finish cleaning the counters and all the tables."

Jeez, maybe her father had been taking pointers from Cinderella's evil step-mother.

"We can help!" Robby said.

A grin split my face. "Good idea, bro!"

Trevor ran behind the counter and grabbed a rag. We all set to work. While my brothers burned some pent-up energy, Vivi spoke quietly to me as we cleaned the back counter together. "My brother called to ask some questions about the family business for his classes. Which led my father and me to argue about my future again. He says I need to study something practical at university, something for our family business."

I scrubbed the counter. "What do you want to study? International travel?"

She hesitated.

I lifted my hands. "Look, no judgement from me, alright? I'm not exactly Mr. University."

She finally said, "I want to study music, but I don't want to go to university. I want to work in the music industry when I grow up. As a singer. Go on tours. But that's not going to happen." Her words rushed out like she was embarrassed. Another first for Vivi. I hated to see her like that.

"You don't know that! That sounds awesome. I didn't know you wanted to do music!" It made sense though—she always sang along with the background music in the shop when she thought no one was paying attention. "So, what kind of music do you like?"

"All of it. Mostly, I love to sing. I can play piano some, but I really want to learn guitar!"

"Get out!" The words burst out, and I couldn't stop the huge smile spreading across my face.

Her eyebrows quirked. "You want me to leave?"

"Ha! No, sorry, I mean, I'm really surprised! I haven't ever heard any playing from upstairs." Their apartment was above the B&B rooms, on the third floor. It was a very small bed and breakfast, with the second floor dedicated to guests, and the gelato shop on the ground floor. Living where she worked allowed for a short commute, but it probably had some downsides, like hearing my brothers argue half the night.

I told her, "For what it's worth, I think that's great!"

"Well, my father feels it's a waste of time." She rolled her eyes. "Especially since he has my life already planned out for me. He's positive he knows exactly what's best for me."

"I guess parents can be like that." Boy, could they ever. *You need to prepare for college, Lucas! That means strong grades in high school! Which means strong grades* now!

"Not yours," Vivi said. "You're always out, seeing new things!" She clasped her hands in front of her chest and gave a wistful sigh.

I didn't have the heart to tell her my wishes had been just as ignored by my parents, but in the opposite direction. They still hoped I was headed for some fancy college like the rest of them, though I think that hope was hanging by a thread these days.

Vivi spun in a circle, dark curls flying. "You get to see the world! And your parents left their professor positions to travel and write a *book*—that's so awesome!"

I wiped the last crumbs from the cone area and tossed them in the trash. "They've actually taken a leave of absence—they're supposed to go back next year."

Vivi smacked one hand on the counter. "Now you're being picky. They made a choice not many would. A brave one! It's so exciting!"

My parents . . . brave? Exciting? More like strange, obsessed with history that was over and done years ago. "Well, traveling the world with my parents isn't as amazing as you might think. Maybe we can trade for a day."

"That'd be so great. I bet they'd let you study music if you wanted to, too."

"Probably." They'd be so happy if I studied *anything* from a classroom.

I glanced at my brothers, busily scrubbing with the same intensity they brought to their grades. The four of them were like a cozy family of brainy bluebirds, and I was this goofy cuckoo stuck in the nest with them. "But we've got who we've got."

Vivi dropped the wipe-cloth and dusted off her hands. "I suppose that's true. It's not worth fighting with him over a crazy dream anyway."

I didn't see what was so crazy about it. I opened my mouth to say so, but she kept going.

She shrugged and smiled. "But at least he gave me permission to go with you to a few more places this afternoon, to make up for the argument, I suppose."

"Awesome! And little brothers are cool to come?"

"Of course!" She sounded like she actually meant it.

We were done in fifteen minutes, the lobby left sparkling. "Thank you, boys!" she said. "You made my day so much better! And now we can go have fun!"

Robby gave me a smug smile. The little jerk. I ruffled his hair.

"Let's do it." I turned to our back-to-bubbly tour guide and held out our special tickets. "Next up: the Sistine Chapel."

CHAPTER NINE
Ol' Mike

The Sistine Chapel was one of the first places my family went when we arrived in Rome, and our tour guide had gotten us in before it officially opened—and it was still crazy crowded. On our way out, the other poor tourists were smashed together like sardines to see it.

The tickets we received must have had their own magic. Not only did we skip the line, but as we walked, extra space appeared on either side of us like a force field. I could get used to this kind of travel. Robby looked around with a furrowed brow, obviously aware that something was different. I pretended not to notice.

When we walked into the chapel, my hands clenched tighter on my notebook in awe. The ceiling soared above us, sixty feet high, full of bright blues, pinks, and yellows. The people up there almost looked like sculptures coming from out of the ceiling, remarkably large and three-dimensional. I craned my neck. "Wow. A) That's a really high ceiling, and B) that's a lot of paintings. How am I supposed to write about all of that?"

Vivi led us to a row of benches along one wall. We sat, better able to support our necks as we gazed upward. "I've read Michelangelo had to lie down on a scaffold to paint this—way up there," Vivi said. "They're actually frescoes. That's why it's lasted so long in such good condition. He painted on top of wet plaster before it dried. Can you imagine?"

I couldn't. My imagination just wasn't enough for something like that. Something so over-the-top big and amazing.

Robby hurried over from reading some display case, hands gesturing wildly and voice about three octaves higher than usual. "These frescos were made with plaster that had volcanic ash from Mount Vesuvius instead of sand, to make it smoother! Michelangelo thought that up himself. That makes him a scientist *and* an artist. How cool is that?!"

It was super cool, and I wished I had been the one to tell Vivi all that. Then I rolled my eyes at my own dart of envy. Robby could grow up to be a professor just like our parents. The smart booger. He'd never fail a class, much less an entire grade. I guess I was proud of him, even if he reminded me of my own total lack.

My gaze flitted from one end of the ceiling to the other, landing on one scene showing what looked like Noah's Ark. The details were hard to see. I lifted my phone and took a zoomed photo . . . and a man in a suit hurried over to me, gesturing to the sign that said no photos were allowed, posted in about eight languages including English.

Whoops! "Sorry—uh, I mean, *scusi*," I said, hurriedly lowering my phone with an apologetic wave. When the guard walked away, I looked down at my photo. It actually looked really good. For such a fast, zoomed-in shot, the focus was sharp, and the framing caught the entire scene right in the center. As I slipped the phone into my pocket, my hand brushed the coin, and heat flashed against my fingertips.

"Uh-oh," I said, pulling out the coin. My brothers were now across the room looking at the big painting of *The Last Judgment* on the far wall. I whispered to Vivi. "If I 'go' anywhere, keep an eye on the boys, okay?"

She nodded quickly. "Of course! I didn't even blink in the time it took you last time. But I'll watch them."

Robby drifted to the middle of the floor, mouth open like a goldfish, staring up at the most famous of all of the pieces: the creation-of-man scene, where God is reaching out to Adam and he's reaching back. Trevor followed, holding Robby's hand. My heart squeezed at the sight of them together like that. I wished I could take a quick shot of them but didn't want to risk the Camera Police. Besides, I had the feeling things were about to get crazy.

I gripped the coin, now hot in my palm, and the lights around me grew brighter and brighter until I had to cover my eyes again. The roar came back, echoing in my ears, and a tremor ran through my body.

It'll be okay, it'll be okay, I chanted to myself, totally not sure it would be okay.

When I opened my eyes, I gasped softly. The ceiling I'd just been staring at with its mammoth figures had changed. This one was only half completed, simply blue with stars on half of it. Colorful, bright frescoes covered most of the other half.

The room was empty except for one other person. An older man, maybe my dad's age, stood on a wooden scaffold attached to the side walls, high in the air. He was hard to see from where I stood, but he was clearly big and muscular with a beard and short wavy hair. After taking a quick glance to confirm no one else was around, I snuck out my phone to use the zoom feature like a telescope. He studied the half-completed scene directly above him, plaster and paint covering his clothes. A cloth hung below the scaffold, also drizzled with paint.

He was muttering under his breath, the sounds whispering past me like ghosts, echoing off the walls. As with my last trip with the coin, language seemed to be no barrier, and I could understand him perfectly. Thank goodness for magic time-travel translation. "I'm a sculptor, not a painter," he was saying, painting on creamy white plaster above him, craning his neck. His face was just a few inches away from the ceiling, yet his artwork was perfectly proportioned as if he was looking from here.

No way. Was that really—? No. Couldn't be. That would be bananas, even for a magic coin.

I stumbled, knocking over a pile of dry brushes, nearly dropping my phone.

The man paused, looked down, and glared. "Who's there? Who are you?"

"Um. I'm Lucas?" I squeaked, shoving my phone and coin

in my pocket. "And you are . . ." I couldn't quite make myself say it. My head felt light.

He wiped his brush on a cloth. "Michelangelo Buonarroti."

It *was* him.

No way. No freaking way.

I swayed on my feet. A chance to talk to the greatest artist of all time? Um, yes, please! It could absolutely save my report—I could even write it like a "creative historical fiction" story! Not even I could screw this up, with a dude as famous as him.

"I was sent to ask you some questions." *I think that's why I'm here, anyway.*

He came down his scaffold one step at a time, wiping reds and blues off his hands on an old rag as he paced toward me. "Who sent you?" His nose was crooked, like someone had punched him. Whoever did that was one brave soul. Possibly crazy.

A woman's voice came from behind me. "I did. Remember me?"

I spun—the green-haired palm reader was with us.

Relief turned my knees to jelly. *I'm not alone back here.* It was amazing how much better I felt knowing she was with me.

Michelangelo stared at her with eyebrows furrowed into a deep V. "You! It's been—"

"Many years, yes, yes." She waved a hand. "And you're welcome. Now tell Lucas about this project. It's important."

He frowned, paint smeared across his forehead. He smelled ripe, but hey, who was I to judge? I was sweating like a maniac again.

"It's really good," I gestured at the ceiling, feeling like an idiot.

"Good is not enough. Consider the Pantheon. Now, *that* is a work worthy of admiration, as if built by angels, not men. I am but a mere mortal," he said.

"But . . . you're super famous," I said, blinking. "You're *Michelangelo*."

He shrugged. "All artists must grow and adapt. For example, at first, my plaster was too wet. It grew mold after I'd completed a section of my fresco. I had to tear that part down and start again. And do you notice the scene with the Ark?"

He pointed to the one I'd taken the illegal photo of before.

"I realized after painting that the ceiling is too high for so many small figures. After that, I decided to make them bigger. Fewer people per scene, but each much larger." He smacked his hand in his fist. "So we can see clearly from here! Like this one, the creation of Eve." He pointed to a woman much larger than the figures in the Ark and flood scene.

Even I could see what he was talking about. Eve demanded the view's attention, whereas Noah got lost in the crowd. "How much longer do you have to go?"

"Two more years, I suspect. By 1512, I hope."

My legs wobbled. I *knew* it, but *hearing* just how far back in time I'd traveled was too wild for words. I looked for reassurance from the palm reader, but she'd disappeared again.

I cleared my throat. "How do you know her? The lady, I mean?"

"The same way you do, I imagine." He crossed his arms with an impatient huff. "Are you facing something difficult in your life? A challenge?"

Gulping I said, "Uh. Yeah!"

"Mmm. My condolences. I didn't want to do this job," he said with a growl. "I have other work to do. But Raphael talked the pope into hiring me instead of him for this job so everyone would see his paintings are better. He's jealous, you see. But I will do my best, even if paint is not my medium of choice."

Wow, I didn't know any of that! "But it's such an important work of art, this ceiling, I mean. It surprises me you didn't want the chance to paint it."

He sat down on a stool nearby and stared at me with dark, intense eyes. They looked like they could bore a hole right through me. "We do not always get to choose the path we are on. We can always, though, choose the way we travel it. I will not crawl when I can march, though my body aches from the work. When I was hired for this job, I told them I must be permitted to do as I liked. Even if some hate my creation, it will be better, coming from my heart. Art requires courage."

Something about his words straightened my back.

He stood, looking upward at the ceiling. "I must work," he said, returning to his scaffold. "Wet plaster is not forgiving. It dries as we speak. Like most things in life, timing is everything."

The light around me began to shimmer, and the coin in my pocket grew warmer. I nodded. "Thank you, Mr. Michelangelo. Sir. It's been an honor."

He turned away without a word. I had not left the room yet, but he clearly didn't see me anymore. His gaze was fastened on his work, determined to make it the very best, taking chances in order to make something of real value. No matter what anyone else thought about it. Even though it hadn't been his idea in the first place.

If that kind of focus was good enough for the greatest artist of all time, maybe it could be good enough for me.

I blinked, the lights flashed, a train roar filled my ears. And then I was back next to Vivi, my brothers chattering, tourists milling, with the completed frescoes above.

"Holy. Cow." I said.

"Where did you go—or when, I guess I should say? I could tell this time—your eyes grew unfocused and your breath grew shallow, and then you took this great big breath—"

"You need to slow down and take a breath, too!" I laughed, so relieved to be home. "I wasn't sure what would happen, but it wasn't nearly as scary as last time, even though Michelangelo is a kinda scary dude."

She did a little hop of excitement. "Oh!" Her voice echoed and several tourists hushed her. She didn't wince, but she did lower her voice. "You met him? For real?"

"As real as time travel can be, I guess. He didn't want to paint this, actually." I gestured at the ceiling. "Can you imagine? He spent four years craning his neck—he stood on a platform, by the way—and worked with super-hard materials to make this, when all he wanted to do was go carve his sculptures. A bummer for him, you know?"

"Well, good thing he didn't get what he wanted, then," she said, gazing upward. "Instead, he made something so beautiful that five million people a year come to see it to be inspired."

I chewed on my lip. "I guess you're right. I hadn't thought about it like that."

Vivi looked around again, hand clutched at her heart almost like it hurt. "I wonder if you could ever bring someone with you. If you travel again."

"Well, it would be a lot more fun than going alone," I told her, and she muffled a squeal behind her hands. "Let's try it next time!"

Maybe it could work. My brothers wouldn't even notice if I took Vivi with me—only a second passed in the current time. I'd ask the magic palm reader next time I saw her.

Pulling out my notebook, I wandered around and read all the little plaques that offered information, taking lots of notes. For the first time, everything here seemed really fascinating. Michelangelo was a real man, after all. With real hopes and dreams, just like me.

Words were pushing against my tongue, like they wanted out onto the page. It was a new experience. I might as well ride the wave. Maybe it would help me write something better than even my last entry. While my brothers and Vivi soaked in more of the Sistine Chapel, I tried to make it come alive for my teachers the way this magic had just done for me.

Dear Ms. Morris, Ms. Deblasio, and Mr. Franklin,

I saw the Sistine Chapel again, and this time I paid attention.

The Sistine Chapel ceiling is mind-boggling. The colors are brighter than you'd think, and the perspective is amazingly accurate, considering that Michelangelo had to paint them up close to be correct from over 60 feet away. The Creation of Adam is super famous and has a lot of memes, so I'm glad to finally get what they're talking about. It was the first time God was shown as a person like that, with all that white hair and the beard. That was a bold artistic choice that was really different than what other people had done. Of course, Michelangelo was a bold dude. Sculptor, painter, architect, scientist. He did it all and looked macho while he did it.

The Last Judgment is the painting behind the altar, and it's huge. I'm talking gigantic. Mary is next to Jesus in her traditional blue fabric, and he's about to smite some guys. It was made later and has a very different vibe from the frescos along the ceiling. Intense and powerful. He even painted his portrait into that scene, as the face of a saint who'd been skinned alive, so . . . yikes, right?

Did you know that he didn't actually lie down on his back to paint the ceiling? He kept notes of how he did it. Not that I wouldn't put it past him to paint lying down, but he made himself a big ol' scaffold and stood on it, 60 feet in the air, craning his neck. Talk about dedication to your art! I think he could have done with maybe a little bit less intensity. But he's made me think . . . I could maybe do with a little more.

He wasn't afraid to put himself or his art out there. When the Pope-the biggest boss man of the Catholic Church-said he wanted the 12 apostles as the subjects of the painting, ol' Mike (I'll call him Mike for short) was like, "Nope, that's totally boring." And then did his own thing. And they let him!

Of course, why wouldn't they? He was THAT good. Like, one in a million kind of good. I guess that's the deal. To have that kind of confidence, it helps to be really good at something. Michelangelo-good. Not many people ever are. I'm sure not. But I did take a few decent pictures today that I'll include with my entry. There aren't many because I found out you can't take pictures inside the chapel. But our day isn't done yet, either.

Sincerely,

Lucas

My journal entry wasn't nearly as informative as an actual trip in time, but it was a step in the right direction. Snapping my notebook shut, I turned to Vivi. "I don't have any other tickets, so it looks like our next trip is on us. Any ideas?"

"He didn't give you any clues?"

I thought back. "He did mention the Pantheon being built by angels or something."

She clapped her hands. "The Pantheon is my favorite ancient building in the city! We don't even need tickets to go—it's free!"

Robby and Trevor came over to see what her fuss was about.

"We're going to our next place," I said.

Vivi crowed, "The Pantheon! It's a famous temple-turned-church, two thousand years old."

She sent me a secret smile. A thrill ran through me. Would I end up going that far back in time again? Would Vivi be able to join me?

She continued, "But first, I think we should stop by one of the most famous works of Michelangelo—the *Pietà*. It's very close, in St. Peter's." She smiled. "I think Michelangelo has left a mark on you, Lucas. We should honor that."

CHAPTER TEN

The Pantheon's Surprise

St. Peter's Basilica was all gold and soaring heights and dimness and seriousness. The dome inside the center was off the charts. People were actually on a walkway up there around the inside rim of the dome, looking down at us, and they looked like ants.

The *Pietà* was off to one side, behind protective glass. This was the famous sculpture of Mary holding Jesus after he died on the cross. I pictured the man I'd just met, coaxing the gentle curves of their bodies from a single piece of marble, and it left me awed.

I took a lot of pictures, just like everyone, but the coin just sat in my pocket, cold. I guess we needed to move on before I would travel again. After all, Michelangelo hadn't mentioned St. Peter's to me—he'd mentioned the Pantheon. Though I felt like St. Peter's could teach a master class on art history or something. My parents had a whole section of their book about it. Now I could see why.

Vivi whispered, "This place is gorgeous, but our next stop is even more amazing to me."

We'd been to the Pantheon the first week we were here, but I couldn't even say what the inside looked like. All I remembered about the outside was that it looked old.

Today, it looked . . . well, still old. The building was smaller than St. Peter's and seriously ancient, but not falling apart like the Roman Forum. From the street, surrounded by taller buildings, the Pantheon looked kind of squashed. It was also sort of dingy along the walls.

This was a big-deal place? Okay, it had its own fountain out front (of course it did), and the columns at the entry porch area were tall, sure, but this wasn't anything like St. Peter's. That place had all the fancy digs. This one was surprisingly plain.

But inside, the Pantheon looked totally different. Surprise! Rounder and fuller than it looked like it should be, it had marble everywhere. It even looked taller than expected.

I sucked in a long, deep breath. The dome at St. Peter's began higher up in the air, but it didn't feel as central to the whole building as this one. In the Pantheon, my eyes were continually drawn up to the dome. It soared over us, filling up the room, checkered with square shapes, with a hole in the center that let in a beam of sunlight and set the place all aglow like some kind of magic portal.

I wrote all this down, fingers trembling. Maybe I could do a whole essay comparing and contrasting the two buildings . . .

Vivi leaned toward me and, in a low voice, explained, "They

think the Pantheon was a temple to all the gods, though there's some debate on that. It was also used for state business meetings and so on. But for sure it's the best-preserved ancient building in Rome. It's been in use for almost two thousand years."

"And it's your favorite ancient spot in Rome?" I asked. She wasn't looking at me. She was totally absorbed in the experience. Her hair looked nearly black in the dim light but shined with reddish highlights where the light touched it. It would have been really pretty for a photograph. The lighting and all.

She smiled up at the bright opening in the center of the dome. "Can't you see why?"

I nodded. Even my brothers seemed humbled, each standing close to me, one on either side. No one running, no one shouting. That didn't last long, though. Just before we reached the center area, Trevor began to fuss.

"I'm tired now. I wanna go home!"

"Shh!" I told him, as a few tourists glared at me. His voice was piercing. I showed him my notebook. "Remember, buddy, I've got to write down a bunch of stuff about this place for my report. You don't want me to fail, do you?"

"But LUCAS!" he said, getting louder.

Vivi squatted beside him. "Do you know why I think they kept this temple to the gods as a Christian church, Trevor?"

He sniffed, rubbing at his eyes. "No."

Robby drew closer, too.

"Because the acoustics are so good."

"Acoustics? What's that?" Trevor was intrigued now, hand dropping to his side.

I was intrigued, too.

She glanced around and smiled mischievously. "Listen." She eyed the ceiling, took two steps away and then sang a series of notes, rising and falling. The notes echoed in the room, amplified by the dome.

Goosebumps prickled down my arms. I didn't know the song, but I didn't care. She sounded amazing. There was no time to record it, but just before she stopped, I caught a snapshot of her, eyes lifted to the ceiling, smiling as she sang.

She looked like one of those Renaissance paintings. But she was prettier than any of the art we'd seen today.

Vivi sang just four or five notes, but they sounded, well, angelic. Haunting. Out of this world. Her soft singing in the shop had always been great, but now it was dialed up a thousand-fold.

This time, her voice took my breath away.

People turned to look, but she turned, too, as if she weren't the one singing. The notes could have come from anywhere, floating in the air all around us.

My brothers stood with their jaws hanging open, any fussing forgotten.

"Talk about magic!" I said before I could stop myself.

She blushed. "Anyone would sound good here." She turned to my brothers. "Feeling better?" she asked Trevor, obviously redirecting the conversation away from herself. "Because we still need to do a few things today."

But my brothers wouldn't let her change the subject.

Trevor put his hand in hers. "You sing real good."

Robby nodded. "You could be famous!"

Her laugh danced around the room like her singing. A couple more shushes came at us, and she clapped a hand over her mouth. "This way!" She pulled me by the sleeve, her other hand still clasped by Trevor's, and camouflaged us among a group of other tourists.

As I snapped shots of the statues, the dome, and the hole in the ceiling (called the oculus, I learned), my mind kept replaying her short song. She was really good. Better than good. But she wasn't going to study music. She was giving up—all that talent, never used. Such a waste.

We followed the curve of the room until we came across a statue of a woman holding a baby. I eyed the name carved on the ground beneath it, then did a double take. "Wait, Raphael is buried here? The famous artist?"

She nodded. "And several Italian kings."

There was a little window in the wall that revealed Raphael's tomb, which held a fancy, ancient coffin called a sarcophagus. His bones were still inside there. Guess it could have been worse—his mummified or wax-covered corpse could have been on display like those old popes in St. Peter's. I had already sent Kei a couple shots of those during my first visit, of course. They looked like haunted house props.

We gazed at the monument. "Kinda creepy, isn't it?" I asked. "To have all these people staring at your tomb?"

She laughed softly. "I guess they thought, why not stay famous?"

"Maybe you'll be that famous one day," I said. Wait. I sighed, closing my eyes. Did I just tell a girl that she might be famous enough to get a stone sarcophagus in the Pantheon one day? *Smooth, Lucas. Smooth.*

When she looked at me blankly, I continued, unable to stop the word vomit pouring from my mouth. "For your music. I mean. You're an artist. Like Raphael, only with songs." I gestured into the air like a fool, miming a symphony conductor.

But she didn't take my words wrong. Amazingly, she seemed to get what I meant even if I had been shoving both feet in my mouth.

She laughed, that bell-like laugh she had. Waggling her dark eyebrows, she said, "Oh sure, I'll live in New York City, and then tour the country with my band."

For once, I wasn't kidding at all. I was dead serious. "Why not? You could. I'll buy your album." Again with the words just spilling out of my face. *Jeez, Lucas, just shut it. She might get the wrong idea.* Like how grown-ups got those weirdly sly smiles on their faces whenever you mentioned a girl's name as a friend. I mean, come on.

Luckily, Vivi didn't blink, though she might have blushed a bit. Too hard to tell in the dim light. "Well, I appreciate your confidence. My family, alas, doesn't share it."

I frowned, holding out my hands. "But maybe if you recorded

yourself—if they'd heard you just now—I should have gotten it on my phone!"

She tucked her hair behind her ears, without meeting my eyes. "It's fine, Lucas. It is what it is. We don't have time to be glum."

Trevor wrapped himself around Robby. "I'm tired."

"Almost ready to go, buddy," I said.

I pulled the coin out, checking for any sign of a glow. Nada. Nothing. Zilch.

"What was the last thing you did before each trip?" she whispered.

I thought back. "Took a picture. I think a photo was the trigger each time, actually. But I took plenty here already." I dropped the coin back in my pocket.

With a deep sigh, she led us all back outside. "Then I guess it's time to go somewhere else. I just really had hoped . . . Give me a second." She walked back to the entrance, taking one last long look inside.

From my place at the edge of the columns, Vivi stood between me and the interior of the building, right in the doorway. The light from inside nearly turned her into a silhouette. Interesting. I lifted my phone and studied the possible shot.

The dimness of the portico roof and gray columns contrasted with the light beyond the heavy metal doors, hinting of something amazing inside. At St. Peter's, everything about it announced it was special. With the Pantheon, you had to do a little looking to see all the good stuff.

I liked the Pantheon better for it.

From where Vivi stood, she had a clear view of both the inside and outside. She looked like she was stepping into a sunlight-filled glade, as if the Pantheon doors were a magical portal.

Click. Examining my photo, I smiled. My art teacher would probably like this one. Maybe. Either way, I definitely did. My chin lifted with pride.

I wished I could've seen the Pantheon in the past. Maybe I could have figured out a way to bring Vivi with me, even without the palm reader's help. If Vivi could travel anywhere, this would be the perfect place. My brothers wouldn't even notice.

Then a familiar heat pressed against my leg. The coin. Trevor and Robby were close, but maybe if Vivi was next to me . . .

"Vivi!" It wasn't too late. I reached my hand out to her, my other pressing against the coin. She met my eyes and ran toward me, arm stretching out.

The coin was getting really hot now.

"Robby!" I said, trying to sound firm without scaring him. "Don't let Trevor wander off, okay?"

He looked at me with his little-old-man look, wrinkled brow, sensing nothing unusual. Trevor was asking to go home. Vivi reached me just as my leg felt like it would go up in flames.

"Here goes nothing!" I said and grabbed her hand.

The light around us grew brighter. My heart raced, and I struggled not to drop the coin or my phone. I couldn't lose all my pictures.

And then came the roar.

Vivi screamed, at least I think she did. The sound filled my ears, and then everything went totally white.

When we opened our eyes, hands still clasped tightly, a bearded man in long robes stood in front of the closed doors—now coated in gold. With a shout, he lifted his arms, and the huge gold-covered doors behind him swung open. Sunlight poured out, bathing him in brilliance.

"Ah!" cried Vivi, stumbling back, throwing an arm across her eyes. After a moment of blinking, my eyes cleared, and the man's silhouette formed against the incredible brightness. I backpedaled but immediately ran into a crowd surrounding the space. Everyone was wearing togas.

Looked like Vivi and I were getting our wish.

The light through the Pantheon doors was totally different now. Brightness had glowed behind them before, but now light was spilling out into the dark porch, reaching out in a celestial spotlight. I didn't even know it was possible from the shape of the building.

"What's going on? With the guy, I mean?" I whispered to Vivi.

A voice behind me answered. "It's April 21."

We both spun and gasped. It was the palm reader, wearing a scarf over the vivid hair this time and more of a robe-style outfit in softer rainbow colors, but definitely her. Thank heavens! Unless she was mad that I brought a stowaway.

The palm reader grinned as if she'd heard my thoughts, her hair as green and white as always where it peeked out from her scarf. "It's a special day for the Pantheon. And for Rome."

Vivi said, "April 21? That's the anniversary of the founding of Rome! It's a huge celebration."

"Correct!" the tattooed lady nodded. "And on this day, every year, the Pantheon is perfectly aligned with the sun so that the light from the oculus shines through its open doors!"

I said, "No, today is May 21."

The palm reader rolled her eyes. "Well, in 126 AD, it's April 21. If you can travel years, why not days?"

Vivi shrieked. "We really just time traveled? Is that what happened? I mean, I KNEW, but . . ." She looked around, eyes wide.

I patted her arm. "It's different when you see it for yourself, right? Don't be scared, though. We've got to keep a low profile here, but we'll be okay."

She grinned—still looking more ashen than usual but with a genuine smile. "Are you kidding? This is AMAZING! I bet we could learn so much. I admit, it feels stranger than I expected." She gulped. "But it's a dream!"

Her excitement was contagious, and I caught myself smiling in response.

The palm reader turned to me. "Mother Rome wanted you to see this moment. Think about why that is." Her eyes danced between Vivi and me. Winking, she said, "Mother Rome knows that travel is better when experienced with the people we care for."

Her words felt layered with meaning, but my brain just wasn't able to keep up. She chuckled and patted my cheek. "Just soak in the moment with Emperor Hadrian here. Rome knows what—and who—you need to hear from."

The man in the robes, apparently Emperor Hadrian, was intoning about the glories of the Roman Empire. Surrounded by light pouring around him from the Pantheon, no wonder people thought he was chosen by the gods to rule. Everything looked a lot shinier today, inside and out.

The light was moving as the sun passed beyond the oculus, already dimming, but the wonder it inspired remained. I said, "That lighting effect . . . it makes the outside match the inside so much more. The outside cleans up really nice."

Vivi's brows drew to a V. "The outside already looks amazing, even in our time! Those tall columns are all one piece, you know! They were shipped by river from Egypt!"

I pursed my lips. "But the outside looks like plain concrete compared to all that fancy space inside."

She scoffed. "It only looks plain to those who don't understand it."

A man in robes behind us tapped me on the shoulder. "I couldn't help but overhear. This entire building is a triumph of architecture, and Hadrian has not hidden all the glory inside. With the marble and shining bronze around the dome—it is dazzling outside as well, is it not? You must have been born in a palace to expect more than such finery."

He looked at my cargo shorts and tennis shoes, frowning. "Though you are dressed most . . . unusually. Perhaps you plan on participating at the footraces at the Stadium of Domitian later . . ." He faded off, caught back up in whatever the emperor was saying.

Vivi whispered, her voice higher than usual, "The building used to have beautiful marble and expensive metals inside and out, but a lot of it got taken to use in other places over the years. It doesn't sparkle quite as much now, but the sunlight still shines out on special days. The Pantheon just needs the right environment to show its full potential."

My throat felt tight, but I had no idea why.

Heat flared from the coin.

"I guess we received our message from 126 AD!" I said, reaching out to Vivi. Her hand was warm in mine.

Her eyes were still on Hadrian, seeming to hold flames inside from the reflection of the doorway light. "I'll never forget this."

"Me either," I whispered. "Quick! Hang on!" I pulled her closer, feeling her weight lean against me.

Vivi's scream followed me into the blinding light, and I realized as the ground solidified beneath my feet that she didn't sound scared. Her scream was of pure excitement.

CHAPTER ELEVEN

Worlds Collide

Back in our time, the doorway was much dimmer, flooded with tourists in jeans and T-shirts and cameras. The gold was gone, but the bronzed doors were just as tall and mighty.

Trevor was fussing at Robby, who was glaring at us with his frustrated look. "Are you just going to ignore us? Trevor's hungry, bro!"

"Sorry!" I gasped. "I got, uh, lost in the moment."

Vivi snorted and turned away to hide her laugh.

Relieved that the boys really were fine, I grabbed Trevor and pulled him close. "Sorry, little man."

I had to reach higher to touch Robby's hand over Trevor's head—he was growing up. He was bigger than he looked at first glance, kinda like the Pantheon. I hadn't noticed until now.

Vivi put a hand to her forehead and whispered so that only I could hear, "We were really in 126 AD, with Hadrian!"

"I'll write about him in my journal." I didn't know enough about him, though, not even from the time trip. But I knew someone who would. "Hey, Robby, what do you know about Emperor Hadrian?"

Robby's frown faded at the attention, not to mention the

chance to show off his smarts to Vivi. "Hadrian rebuilt the Pantheon, you know," he replied. "I mean, he didn't do it by hand, but he planned it—the largest unsupported cement dome in the world. Not one beam of metal supports the dome. It's incredible."

Vivi chewed on her lip for a moment. "Was this building actually inaugurated on April 21, do you know?"

She was asking me, but Robby answered, saving me from looking ignorant. "I haven't read anything about an exact inauguration date, but based on the design of the dome—"

Trevor cut him off. "What's that mean? In-og-a-rated?"

Finally, a question I could answer. "Inauguration is when a building is brand new and gets a big kickoff when it opens. Like when they opened the new college library, and Mom gave the speech?"

Trevor shook his head, but I remembered it like it was yesterday.

My parents' coworkers kept saying things to me like, "How's school going? Bet you're taking all honors, huh, with parents like yours?"

I had nodded and felt heat creeping along my face. I'd totally lied. I hadn't been in any honors classes. Regular classes had been plenty hard for me (and they still were). I hadn't wanted my parents to have to explain the mystery of how I turned out completely unlike them.

But I'd bet none of those supersmart people had ever seen

the light glowing in the doorway of the Pantheon on the spring equinox. And they sure didn't see it in way back in time.

No one would ever believe it, not even Kei. I met Vivi's eyes and wrapped an arm around each brother. Well, at least she believed me. She'd lived it, too.

As we left the Pantheon behind, weaving among the crowded sidewalks, Vivi brushed hair from her face and leaned close. "That. Was. Amazing. Thank you! I hope I can travel with you again. What were you doing just before . . . we left?" She glanced at my brothers.

Thinking back was hard. It felt like years ago already. *Let's see.* We were almost leaving, I saw the light, noticed Vivi in the doorway . . .

"Oh! I took picture of, um, the Pantheon's doorway," I held out my camera, adding hastily. "While you were standing in it." It wasn't a close-up, like I'd wanted to take at the Colosseum that time, so I didn't think it was too weird to show.

Her cheeks turned rosier than usual. "It's a really artistic shot. I don't even recognize myself."

In this last shot before our time trip, Vivi's stance mirrored the emperor's, almost. And the image showed off the power of the building. It hinted at the inside, made the viewer want to see more. It was a good photo, almost like a piece of art.

Or something.

Not that I was Michelangelo.

But I had wanted to capture this place and its history, and I kinda thought I had. This place made me want to show it off.

I bet Mom and Dad feel like that when they write about the history of a place.

The new thought left me blinking.

Well, maybe I could try reading their book one day. Or at least talk about it with them. Learning more about places I'd traveled actually sounded . . . fun. And so did taking pictures of them. I'd had fun today.

But . . . "I had taken other pictures here, too. Plenty of them," I said. "I don't know why this one sent us back." I showed her all the ones I'd taken inside.

"Wow, all your photos are really wonderful!" she said. "You should post these somewhere else besides a report. These belong out in the world."

I smiled at her enthusiasm. "Maybe." No way, but I didn't need to say that and bum her out. She'd forget about me soon enough after I left.

Eying the shot with raised eyebrows, Vivi said, "You probably think you'll leave and I'll forget."

Busted. She knew me better than I thought. I couldn't stop the laughter from escaping.

She pointed a finger. "Well, I won't forget. We'll find a way to show off your work one of these days. More than just a school project, too." She poked me in the shoulder.

I just grinned and shook my head.

Trevor started fussing, and we picked up the pace to get home before he had a full meltdown. Then I'd work on my journal tonight before I forgot everything.

Excitement bubbled up inside of me. I was looking forward to writing something. That was a first.

"We've really done a lot today," I said. "Tomorrow is our last full day here. Do you think you could go with us again, Vivi? With or without my parents?"

"I'll ask," she promised. "Sundays are busy, but this is a special occasion."

Her smile left me feeling warm.

The rest of the walk back to the B&B was quiet, each of us lost to our own thoughts.

"Thanks," I said to Vivi at our front door as my brothers thundered inside. "And you agree we should keep all this just between us, right? The time travel stuff, I mean?" Signora Russo's warning rang in my head.

Vivi snorted and said, "If you think I'm telling my father I traveled through time, you have not met my father! I'm not telling *anyone*, don't worry. I don't fancy the thought of talking to a psychiatrist."

Good. My phone dinged. KEI CALLING.

Perfect timing! I glanced at Vivi—she'd wanted to meet him. "I know you can't stay long, but do you want to meet Kei?"

I should probably warn Kei first that Vivi was there . . . he might joke about the horse-butt shots or worse. I'd have to talk fast.

She grinned. "The famous Kei? Of course!"

"Come on in." Inside, it smelled like my parents had reheated lasagna for an early dinner to eat while they worked. They did that a lot.

"Mom! Dad! We're back!" I called. "Vivi's with me!"

I answered the phone and said, "Hang on a sec, Kei!"

Trevor ran into the living room yelling to our parents, "We saw lots and Vivi sang and it was awesome!"

Dad adjusted his glasses and chuckled. "Sounds like you had quite an adventure."

I stifled a laugh. "That's for sure."

Relieved that no further questions were asked and that the boys were busy badgering my parents for food, I led Vivi to my desk. Instead of using my phone, I opened the app on my laptop. Kei's face looked gigantic on the computer screen.

"Dude!" I said to him. "Good to see your ugly mug!" His skin was bronzed from sunburn along his cheekbones and nose. He'd been practicing soccer a lot, I bet.

"Right back at you!" He grinned.

"So, hey, there's someone I want you to meet—"

But he was barreling on. "Hey, listen, I called because the high school soccer coach visited our team today."

All other thoughts poofed away. "And?" I leaned forward.

Kei said, "Get this. He's starting a freshman summer soccer camp! It's going to be a requirement for anyone trying out for the freshman team. Kids who move in after summer are exempt, but you and I will both have to go."

That sounded cool, actually. I needed to get into shape anyway. "How long will it last?"

He shrugged. "I don't know, but it's running at the same time as summer school, so I guess a while?"

Same time as summer school.

Dread pooled in my stomach. "So . . . if someone had to go to summer school to make up a failing grade, theoretically, they wouldn't be able to try out for the team even if they passed, because they couldn't go to soccer camp?"

"That's what it sounded like, yeah. Why? You looking at summer school or something? I thought you were doing okay?"

I glanced at Vivi, and she watched me with those big dark eyes. She understood the real deal. But I really didn't want to get into it right now.

"Nah, I'll be okay. Just . . . thinking." Kei knew I wasn't a stellar student. I mean, everyone knew that. But failing suddenly felt so much more real, even with all the magical help. It wasn't like the palm reader lady was giving me a new brain to write with or something, and I wasn't sure if what I was writing was what my teachers would like.

I guess deep down, I'd assumed that even if I didn't do so hot with my report, I'd scrape by one way or the other with summer credits. And now that option was gone—or soccer was, which would ruin high school anyway.

I really had to pass eighth grade. No second chances now. Crap.

"This must be Kei," Vivi rescued me, stepping into the frame.

I nearly jumped out of my skin. It felt weird to have my best friend meet my new friend here. And vice versa. Especially when one was really pretty and I didn't know what the other might say to her. The feeling made me my stomach feel jittery.

"Kei, Vivi. Vivi, Kei," I made belated, rushed introductions. I hadn't been joking when I told her we wouldn't have long to talk. Especially on a Saturday, Kei would have places to go, people to hang out with—people who weren't me.

"I've heard good things about you," Vivi said politely, sounding very grown up and European.

Kei's ears turned deep red to match his burned face. Jeez, what a goober, always liking the pretty ladies. "Uh, well, thanks? Did y'all go sightsee more today?"

"Vivi helped me out, yeah." I said, nodding my head at Vivi in thanks.

She said to Kei, "Wait till you see some of the shots he got today! He's quite the talented photographer, our Lucas."

Our Lucas.

The words stole my ability to argue about her calling me a talented photographer. Kei's lip quirked up—dear God, he'd call me *Our Lucas* forever now.

I hastily changed the subject. "Did you know they used to make people fight lions in the Colosseum?"

Kei snorted. "Duh, yeah, there's plenty of movies about that."

"Oh! I should look them up! I could find other movies set in Rome, too—add them to my journal. Which is your favorite?" I asked. No one knew movies like Kei. He'd introduced me to a bunch of cult classics.

Vivi checked her phone. "I'll leave you boys to your

movie-talk." She hesitated and gave me a little wave. "See you tomorrow, Lucas."

"For sure."

She slipped out the door. I could practically see Kei's determination to dig up all the intel on her—but I didn't want to talk about her when she wasn't here. She wasn't just some girl Kei was thinking about asking out. She was my friend.

A really nice friend who happened to be a pretty girl, that's all.

Before he could spit out a word, I asked, "What movies should I watch?"

As expected, Kei leaned back, hands behind his head, and kicked his feet up on his desk. "Listen and learn, my friend."

I ended up jotting down a handful of movies and TV shows set in Rome. I bet I could weave some old classic movies in and really impress my teachers.

And I really had to impress them *a lot*. Those magic trips were the only thing saving my bacon at this point, especially now that scraping my way into high school over summer was off the menu. Not that summer school would've ever been fun, but I couldn't risk losing the soccer team next year.

Visions of me alone at an empty lunch table for the next four years flooded my mind. It was bad enough to miss playing this spring, but to mess up my chances for high school . . .

Kei picked at the edge of his sleeve. "You look pretty tired, man. I guess it's a lot of walking, huh? Your legs must be getting a good workout!"

"Not as much as you might think—we take a lot of breaks for the little dudes. Today was okay. I got some decent pictures. No toilet shots, though."

Should I send some of my real pictures to him? My fingers hovered over the one of the Pantheon and Vivi, but I put the phone in my pocket instead.

Instead I said, "And walking can get tiring, but it's nothing like soccer practice, you know? I'm out of shape. So even if I get to go to the soccer camp, the coach might wonder why I bothered."

Kei waved off my concern. "No way! You're a great player. But you know, if you don't make the team for whatever reason, you could still hang out with us, be the water boy or something?" He studied the ceiling as he said that last part, his face unnaturally blank.

A knot filled my throat, and I flinched. The *water boy*? The unfairness burned like fire in the back of my eyes. I blinked hard. "We'll see. Thanks for the heads-up about the camp. I've got one last big project to go."

Kei nodded, looking brighter. "You've got this. I still can't believe they're making you do homework there, but your toilet seats should have their own blog, you know. Genius art, really."

We laughed. "Thanks. I'd better go. The sooner I get this thing written, the better."

Kei glanced at his phone and winced. "Yeah, I gotta go, too."

"Is everything going okay on your end of things?" I'd been so freaked out, maybe I'd missed something.

"Yeah, but you know, Leslie got mad at me for not taking her out to the movies last week."

"Wait, you're going out with Leslie Brenner?" My head spun. What else was I missing out on, being so far away? What else would I miss if I couldn't fix the tryout situation?

"Nah, we went out once, but she doesn't like anything I do. But now she wants to talk all the time. Hey, you make sure you get that Italian girl's number before you go." He waggled his eyebrows in his goofy way, as if I'd be asking her out any minute now.

"Vivi?" My stomach did a funny little dance at her name. "We're just friends."

"Whatever, my dude. At least enjoy your time with her until you have to say *adios!*"

"I think you mean *ciao.*"

He rolled his eyes. We both laughed and ended the call.

We'd be okay, me and Kei. But saying goodbye to Vivi really wasn't a funny thought at all.

CHAPTER TWELVE

Time to Get Serious

Focus was the name of the game now. All this time travel wouldn't help me if I couldn't put stuff into words for my teachers. I let thoughts of my conversation with Kei fade away. I'd had good luck lately writing my entries by hand, so I'd do that and then type it all up later before I turned it in.

My room was a tiny bed and the miniature dresser next to the window—pretty much a closet, but cozy. Gazing out at the late-evening blue of the sky, I shook out my arms and sat on the bed. The clock on the wall ticked loudly. My brothers were playing together peacefully in their room, a miracle almost as amazing as time travel.

Was today real? Had I really stood in the dusty air of the Colosseum in ancient Rome? Talked with Michelangelo? Traveled back to the Pantheon in 126 AD? My head felt like a slushie inside.

Luckily, I had plenty to say this time, thanks to Vivi—and Mother Rome, I supposed. I even had a poem in mind. I opened up my notebook and grabbed a fresh pencil.

Dear Ms. Morris, Ms. Deblasio, and Mr. Franklin,

Did you know that the Pantheon has been built three times? Guess the third time's the charm, because the third building has lasted for over 1800 years.

The neatest thing about the Pantheon is that the inside is a total surprise. The outside looks kinda squat and plain, but inside, it's full of open space and fancy marble and statues. It used to be fancier, but as a friend pointed out, lots of stuff got taken to decorate other things. It's still impressive just the way it is.

Michelangelo called the Pantheon a work of angels, which is really saying something. In fact, when Mike made the dome for St. Peter's in the Vatican, he kept his dome five feet smaller than the Pantheon as a sign of respect. He was one classy dude.

I think Michelangelo is probably my favorite artist of all time. He was an Artist with a capital A, no fears and no apologies. Putting your art out there like that takes a lot of guts.

In St. Peter's, we saw one of his most famous works, the Pietà. It's kept behind a triple layer of bulletproof glass (they are not messing around!). Mike was only 23 years old when he made it. He showed every muscle and each fold of clothing, making marble look soft.

It's the only piece of his art that he signed. I can see why he'd want to be sure people knew he'd created it. I wish I could make something even a fraction as beautiful. I did, though, get a few shots of the Pietà I'm proud of. I also wrote a poem about the Pantheon. It's nothing fancy, but it's a serious one (shocking, I know!).

Inside/Outside

A perfect sphere is hidden inside
With light and air and color,
Hidden beneath gray concrete years ago.

No one knows how the dome was made
So heavy, impossibly solid but curved.
But they left a hole
For light to shine inside

And sometimes,
When the timing is right
The light spills out the doors.
Onto our feet, inviting us to seek
The surprise waiting within.

A deep satisfaction flooded me. I wrote a poem. I mean, it might not be great, but it was definitely a poem. And not so bad. Who knew it was possible?

Not Ms. Sala, my third-grade teacher. She once gave me an F on a poem about a big purple dog eating a planet on a stick. She said it failed because it didn't fit the assignment, but I stopped writing poems after that. Maybe I'd send her this poem one day.

I gasped when I checked the time. Already eleven p.m.? I'd been working steadily for three hours. Time had really flown, no magic or time travel required. Just focused concentration.

I stretched my back, feeling good.

Robby knocked on the wall next to my little bed. "Hey, today was cool." He shifted foot to foot, not quite meeting my eyes in a hesitant and very non-Robby-like manner. "So, tomorrow, Trev and I can still come with you, right? If you hang with Vivi again?"

Feeling generous in my good mood, I said, "Look at that sad puppy dog face." I reached out, yanked him down, and gave him a noogie. "What would I do without all your facts, man? Half the stuff I wrote tonight was because of you and your boy-genius!"

His face grew pink, but his smile faded. "I don't know why you do that."

"Do what?"

"Put yourself down all the time."

I pushed the hair out of my eyes. "It's not an insult if it's true."

He shook his head, lips turned down. "Well, I don't like you talking about my brother that way, so knock it off." This time he rumpled my hair, as if he were the big brother or something.

"Whatever, little dude." Shaking off the gooey emotions, I moved to my desk. "I'm not sure where Mom and Dad want to go tomorrow, but maybe you can help me with something . . ." I grabbed my notebook. "I took some, uh, notes about a place where Romans might have held footraces or something. I wrote down 'The Stadium of Dom-something.' Does that ring any bells?"

Robby puffed out his cheeks. "Stadium of Domitian, I think? I don't know much about it."

I laughed. "Well, we're in the same boat for once."

Clacking quickly on the keyboard, I pulled up some Rome sites. "Looks like . . . wow, that's a really old place that used to hold the Roman Olympics!"

Robby, unable to resist, read over my shoulder, double-speed. "Oh, the Piazza Navona was built over it eventually! We went there the first week but must have missed that museum. I'd definitely remember an ancient Olympics museum. Oh my gosh, that would be awesome to see!"

It definitely would—especially since I bet the clue from the Pantheon guy meant I'd time travel if we went there. So I'd have to make sure we did. "Then tomorrow will be your lucky day, Smurf. We'll just need to convince Mom and Dad."

Seeing the ancient Olympics would be fantastic for my report.

Robby bowed. "As you say, so shall it be, oh great Sibling the First."

I rolled my eyes. "Get out of here, you weirdo."

He laughed and trotted away. Before he pulled the curtained area closed, he said, "Um. Thanks, Lucas. For bringing us today. I'll never forget everything we saw."

A sudden swamping of brotherly affection made eyes sting

and throats feel funny. Emotions were sticky, man. Shaking it off, I dug a little deeper online on the Piazza Navona and the Stadium of Domitian.

This time, I wanted to be prepared if I got thrown back in time. And as shocking as it was to admit, my research made for really interesting reading.

When I woke up in the morning, the crazy events of the day before seemed like a dream, the kind of story Trevor would tell after he woke up too early. I shook my head but then looked over my journal entries and photos . . . I really had been to those places.

There was no evidence of our time trip, of course, but my journal entries spoke for themselves. I'd never written so well before. And my pictures were looking pretty sharp. Now I just had to keep up the good work. Hopefully more time trips were in store for today.

I tucked the coin in my pocket, patted it once, and said, "Okay, let's see what Rome has in store for us today."

At breakfast downstairs, Vivi's eyes were sparkling with excitement. As she set out some more cut-up fruit, she leaned over and whispered. "Father said I could go with you today. Since it's your last full day to sightsee."

Her breath against my ear combined with the words *last day* made my chest feel strangely tight. I managed a smile. "Perfect!"

"I still can't believe it was real. But it was, right?" Her toes tapped a steady rhythm even when she stood still, and her dimples popped with suppressed laughter.

I grinned at her obvious delight. "It was."

Dad set down his tablet. "So, how's your journal coming along, Lucas? Today's pretty much your last chance for research. Is there anything missing you need to fill in?"

Perfect opening for my pitch. I said, "This morning, I'd really love to go back to Piazza Navona." I cleared my throat and added, "If that's okay with you. It's pretty famous and all, and has an ancient Olympics museum right there."

Robby gave me a conspiratorial thumbs-up.

Dad pushed up his glasses in excitement. "Piazza Navona? Well, that's perfect, because your mother and I need to do a little more interviewing with our source there."

He wasn't even getting on my case for not paying attention the first time, thank goodness.

I asked, "Vivi can still come, right?"

My mom lifted her head to study me.

"Of course!" Dad said.

I was sure that it wouldn't be awkward at all. At least my parents' big brains were always thinking about the *past*. Maybe they could help my project, too. Though they could stand to be a little more focused on NOW.

My mom said, "Actually, I think Piazza Navona would be better this afternoon, don't you think, honey?" She put her hand on my dad's. "Maybe Lucas and Vivi could go to some other places this morning together and save that one for after lunch, with us?"

"What about us?" Robby demanded.

I opened my mouth to say they could join us, but my mom smoothly said, "I have some work for you to help with me, Rob. But we'll all go out together this afternoon."

He frowned but didn't complain. And when I nudged his foot with mine, he gave me a reluctant eye roll. We'd be okay.

I didn't know why my mom was suddenly chill with me hanging out with Vivi, but I wasn't about to ask her why. Vivi made a great traveling buddy, no matter where we went. Or when. I'd never met anyone with such joy about everyday stuff.

Vivi and I stepped out of the gelato shop. She clapped her hands with a little squeal. "Okay, then! Let's do this! Where do you think Rome wants you to go now? Or should I say 'Mother Rome'?"

I ran a hand through my hair. "Well, the clues for the next trip have always seemed to be mentioned in the past. But the hint was about Piazza Navona, I'm almost sure, so I don't know what to do until then. Your guess is as good as mine."

"Maybe the palm reader will be at the fountain and we could ask her?"

"Good thinking," I said, tucking my notebook in my pocket, ready to go. The coin was back in my side pocket, buttoned up safe.

As always, we heard the fountain before we saw it. Smelled

it, too—that sort of half-chemical and half-humidity smell that came from such a large fountain in a small square.

The tattooed palm reader was there, on the far side of the square, wearing her handwritten sign. Relief flooded me, as well as an unexpected warmth, like I was running into an old friend.

"Hey!" I called to her as we jogged over. "My parents delayed our next tourist spot to this afternoon—do you have any advice for how to spend our morning?"

She winked. "I always have advice." Her gaze turned to Vivi. "Ah. Hello, Viviana."

Vivi jumped a little next to me. The woman reached over and grabbed her hand.

"Um, excuse me?" Vivi said, but the palm reader was staring down at her palm like the lines were written in plain English. Or Italian, maybe.

"Yes, see, right here? You, Vivi, are happy to help others take risks, but it's about time for you to open new doors for yourself."

Vivi sniffed, clearly a bit put out. "I'm not afraid to try new things!" She looked at me for confirmation. I nodded.

The palm reader said, "We all have something we're hiding." Her gaze lifted. "Both of you must be honest with those who matter most if you want to move forward in life."

Vivi and I exchanged a glance, and I shrugged.

The palm reader dropped Vivi's hand and gave a long sigh. "I see my words have fallen upon hard soil. It might take a bit of rain to soften you both up. In the meantime, Vivi, show him *your* Rome."

Vivi's brow furrowed. "*My* Rome?"

The woman patted Vivi's cheek. "You've got time for two places this morning: the place you go to dream and the place you go to think."

Vivi's eyes lit up. "You mean I get to show Lucas some of my favorite places?" She spun to me. "Would your teachers want you to write about those, do you think?"

I chewed on my lip a minute. On the one hand, I really needed to write about lots of history from a serious perspective for my classes. This was it. My last day in Rome.

But that also meant it was my last day with Vivi. She was still smiling at me—and I couldn't help but smile back. "Well, it would sure be insider's knowledge of Rome, right?"

And the way the palm reader was slyly smiling, she had more than one trick up her tattooed sleeve.

Vivi's grin grew even wider, like a Cheshire cat's. "Exactly. So, I'll show you my favorite spots before you go. And when I come to Austin one day, you can show me around yours. Deal?"

When I come to Austin one day . . .

I nodded, suddenly unable to find any words.

Vivi turned back to the palm reader. "Wait! Would this coin work in other places, too? Like Austin? Or New York? Or Barcelona? Or—"

The palm reader waved her hand. "Sorry, but no. This coin is tied to this city alone, and its magic lasts only until the wish is completed. Enjoy it while you can, young ones."

"Shall we go enjoy a magical day, then?" Vivi asked me with a giggle.

I smiled. "My favorite kind."

We headed down a long street close to the big white square building with a super-tall statue of a guy on a horse. I'd visited there with my family last week but I didn't remember what it was. The streets were packed with little cars.

Vivi took a sudden turn into a tiny alley—or was it a road? Hard to tell sometimes and pointed to some stairs that seemed to lead to nowhere. There wasn't a building above us, that was for sure.

"What? We're going up there?"

"Trust me," she said.

I climbed the steps, which went up one level, turned, and then landed at the top.

We walked into a hidden green park, a full story above the street below. "Whoa. What is this place?"

"This garden is open to the public, but most tourists never find it. It's peaceful, yes?"

I nodded. "Very."

A walled sidewalk ran along the edge of the park, allowing a view of the traffic below, but once I stepped back into the green space, all of that fell away. Flowers and orange trees dotted the spaces between graveled pathways, with benches spaced along the path. A small fountain—of course—was in the center.

We sat in the shade at the edge of the park, overlooking the big white building down the street. Behind us, a couple walked three dogs in a tangle of leashes. A young family sat on another bench at the end of the path.

As we lounged under the shady trees, Vivi told me a little about the big white building, called the Victor Emmanuel II Monument. She said it'd be good for my report, since I admittedly didn't remember much about it from our trip there.

"It's unofficially called 'the wedding cake,'" she added, outlining the shape in the air with her hands. "Because it's so frilly and frothy with grandeur. Sometimes, it's called 'the typewriter'—for the shape—or even 'the dentures.'" She giggled.

"That's clever." So was sightseeing from a distance like this. It was sure a lot easier on the legs. One thing I did remember about our visit there was all the steps the monument had.

I took a deep breath and leaned my head back. Patches of deep blue sky looked like jewels through the leaves. "And I'm really glad you showed me this park," I said. "It's so peaceful, like its own little world."

She looked around, taking it all in. "I feel the same. It's not a famous landmark, but it's my favorite place for dreaming. I'm glad you like it." She stood and dusted off her pants. "Next up—my place for thinking."

As we headed back down the stairs to the street level, I realized I hadn't even taken a picture of the park. In this hidden space of green and quiet, I'd finally felt . . . relaxed. Normal. "Wait," I said. "I want to remember that place, out of all of Rome."

She was already two steps ahead. She paused and looked back over her shoulder. "What?"

"Nothing," I said. And my feet carried me forward. I didn't need a photograph to capture this moment forever.

CHAPTER THIRTEEN

A Realization

Two blocks later, we turned down a narrow road cluttered with bicycles leaning against the stone walls and little flower pots hanging outside windows.

"There's a bookstore over here that I love," she said. "It's a secondhand shop and is my favorite—my dad showed it to me. He used to spend hours here, until life got too busy. It's got so many books, you could never be lonely. Over a million!"

She pointed toward a blue-and-silver awning over a narrow door that looked barely big enough to fit through. "That place holds a million books? I guess looks can be deceiving."

"It's all about working with what you have," she replied with arched eyebrows.

A boy our age, maybe a little older, was sitting at a table near the shop with a tiny cup of espresso, scrolling through his phone.

"David!" she called. She sounded surprised—and pleased.

He looked up and smiled. He said something to her in Italian, sounding like some cool leading man in a movie. Italian basically sounds like a spontaneous love sonnet every time someone opens their trap. I didn't know who this David guy was, but I didn't like him.

Vivi tugged my hand with hers, leading me. "Come, I want you to meet a friend of mine! It'll just take a minute."

Great.

But her hand was warm in mine.

"David, this is Lucas. Lucas, David."

"Uh. Hi," I said. Because I'm brilliant like that.

She hadn't let go of my hand. I didn't let go, either. Should I? What was happening? We weren't time traveling, and she didn't need help to steady herself. She was just . . . holding my hand. In front of this other guy.

She squeezed my hand, just a little.

My palm felt electrified, but she looked completely chill. Maybe for Italians, holding hands with a guy friend was a thing they did all the time.

David stood. Jeez, he was a lot taller than I thought. Like a football player, an American one. Last week in Florence, I'd seen a famous statue called *David*, by my main dude Michelangelo. The statue *David* was seriously ripped, total muscles, like he was designed to make every other guy in the room feel like a wimp.

I bet this David was named after that statue. Figured he'd be friends with Vivi.

David-in-the-flesh looked me over, pausing over where Vivi's hand still clasped mine, but his face didn't change. "*Ciao.*"

I nodded at him and wished I knew how to say "Nice to meet you" in Italian. With Vivi's English so strong, it had been easier just to stick with that than try to learn Italian. Maybe she could teach me some words later. That would impress my teachers. And it would be cool to share with Vivi, too.

"Are you new here, Luca?" David asked. He'd switched to English for me. Which was nice, admittedly.

"It's Lucas. And just passing through," I said.

He nodded but didn't correct himself. "Well, I hope you have a good holiday." He offered his hand, like we were grown-ups or something, and I had to pull mine from Vivi's to shake his. Just as well. My palms were beginning to sweat.

"His parents are researching for a book. Lucas is an American," Vivi offered, which I thought seemed plain enough from my English greeting, since it wasn't like I sounded British.

I glanced at her out of the corner of my eye. She told David about showing me the garden, but there was no flush to her cheeks or any kind of glow to her eyes. Wasn't there supposed to be a glow when a girl liked someone? Or maybe I was just missing it because I didn't want to see those feelings there, for him.

Oh my gosh. I sucked in my breath as the truth bomb landed like a punch to the face. I was irritated by David because I was *jealous.* I was afraid Vivi might see him as boyfriend material.

And I wanted her to see *me* like that.

I liked holding her hand. Making her happy made me feel like a superhero. I kept noticing how pretty she was. Holy cow, I *like-liked* her.

After all of my "We're just friends," too. I'd been fooling myself, afraid of what it would mean.

There was no denying it, not after just holding her hand

turned me stupid. Lucas Duran had finally fallen for a girl. And I was leaving tomorrow. I'd probably never see her again.

And besides, who was I kidding? I was so clueless, even if I were staying, I'd have no way of knowing if she *liked* Football David.

Or me.

"I was just going to show Lucas the bookstore." She tilted her head, looking ridiculously cute. "Want to come in with us?"

Please don't, please don't, I begged silently.

He slurped down the rest of his espresso—of course he drank espresso, he probably ate pure iron, too—and said, "*Grazie.* Sounds fun." I swear the sunlight glinted off his teeth.

Unfortunately, David joined us, gesturing Vivi ahead of him like a friggin' knight in shining armor.

Yeah, I *really* didn't like David. He was totally messing up my last chance alone with Vivi, maybe ever. She didn't even know how I felt. To be fair, *I* had barely figured out how I felt.

It was just at that moment that Vivi grinned at me, and it was like fireworks inside me.

I should tell her. The thought struck like lightning, bright and terrifying and powerful. That must have been what the tattooed palm reader meant. Why she sent us here. To kick me in the rear.

My mind was spinning a million miles per hour. It wasn't just that Vivi was really pretty. I mean, she was, and I'd noticed. Duh.

But Vivi was special. It was all of her: her jokes, her bubbly enthusiasm, and her passion for music. The way she encouraged me and believed in me. She helped me see the world in a brand-new way.

And I was leaving tomorrow.

The pang in my chest was unexpectedly harsh.

Well, David or no David, Vivi and I had the rest of the day together, so I'd find the perfect moment, and then I'd tell her how I felt.

Though I might skip writing a poem on that.

There were some things about Rome my teachers just didn't need to hear about.

When we ducked through the bookshop's entrance, a little bell over the door rang and the smell of paper and coffee surrounded us. Vivi and David greeted the bookstore owner, who waved back from the register.

Stuffed bookshelves lined the walls, with a couple of small tables and chairs in the center. The checkout counter was covered tiny framed postcards from all over the city. The second floor held books for kids, and toys spilled out from a trunk to keep little ones happy. The shop was small, but full of the happy chatter of customers.

My parents would be in heaven here. Robby, too. I was actually a bit bummed he was missing it. Here was a slice of everyday Rome, captured in this one little shop. I took a few photographs, but the coin didn't heat up, not even a bit.

Vivi pulled one paperback after another from a shelf, pointing at covers that were faded or scrawled on. It was all really cool. Even if David hovered nearby, reading titles in Italian like a show-off.

"Do they have English books?" I asked.

She smiled. "They do! Maybe you want one for the plane ride back? I'm so jealous of all the time you've spent traveling!"

"Don't be. Traveling all the time can be really lonely." The words slipped out, and I stifled a sigh. I wasn't about to bare my soul with David lurking around.

She studied me. "Even here?"

I felt my cheeks light up. My face probably looked like a stop sign. "No, of course not. Rome has been . . . different."

Tell her, Lucas.

Her smile flashed again. "Then we're doing something right. And now we'll get you a book to take with you. The English books are right over here. You should take some notes for your journal, too! This will be good stuff!"

The moment slid right by. *Strike one!*

I jotted down all sorts of things about the bookstore. It had been around for generations. How cool that Vivi's dad used to hang out here as a young man. I wondered if my parents had thought to ask him about that for their book. Maybe he knew some special history.

I even wrote down a short, silly poem. Who said that all poems had to be deep?

There once was a bookstore in Rome.
So Roman it lacked only a dome.
With shelves stuffed with books
And lots of fun nooks,
It demanded its very own poem.

I laughed out loud to myself. My teacher was going to dig that one. We browsed some more and I stayed close to Vivi, constantly aware of her presence, like a physical magnet pulling at me in a way I hadn't noticed before.

"Here is it!" she squealed. "My favorite book, in English! You must let me get this for you as a going-away present!" She held out a copy of *A Wrinkle in Time* by Madeleine L'Engle.

I'd read it once for class a while back. Well, pretended to read it, goofing off most of the time. "What do you love about it?"

"What's not to love? She travels across the universe to save her father! She visits different worlds! She's strong and determined! And it all ends up happily ever after!"

I took the thin book, thumbing through its pages without seeing the words. No wonder she loved this story. Vivi wanted an adventure. But unlike this book, her dad was the one standing in her way.

"Thanks," I said. "I'll make sure Robby reads this when I'm done." I'd really read it this time, too.

"And Trevor—I bet he'd like it, too," she said. "You could read it to him. Ooh, maybe we can find him a little toy." She wandered off, exploring the shelves, exclaiming now and then with delight. That openness to discovery and joy was the way she seemed to approach everything—except her own dream. I wished I could help her like she'd helped me.

Before we left, I needed to make a pit stop in the store's bathroom. It had been a long morning. I stuffed my new book in my pocket with my journal—it was a tight fit, but I hadn't expected any gifts today. "I'll meet y'all out front in a minute."

The tiny door squeaked open to reveal a bathroom barely big enough to turn around in, with a naked bulb hanging above the john. The toilet was rectangular!

A grin lit my face: a new shape to add for my secret weird toilet photo collection. But the best part was that the toilet seat itself was covered with images of the statue of *David*. No kidding, the celebrated statue had his own toilet seat.

That was some fame, right there. This had to be seen to be believed. I pulled out my phone.

I snapped a picture with a snicker. Kei was getting this one for sure.

It was a nice break to have some goofy fun with my photos again. My new photos made me proud, but I liked to laugh, too. That would never change.

Wait, why was the room getting brighter?

The coin. The coin was on fire—here, in a freaking bathroom. *You've got to be kidding me.*

Out of all the photos I'd taken this morning, *this* was the special one that was going to send me back in time? Here? Alone?

I blinked, and when I looked around, the bathroom still stood around me, but the *David* seat cover was gone.

Carefully, I opened the door.

It looked much the same. The little bell over the front door chimed, and a young guy walked in, someone who looked familiar. Maybe sixteen years old, maybe twenty, hard to know.

The manager said, in perfectly translated English, "Good to see you today, Mr. Bonacelli."

Bonacelli? That was Vivi's last name.

I stared, unable to help myself, as the young man settled himself at one of the little tables, pulled out a notebook, and began to write. He looked really familiar, but I couldn't quite place him. Was he maybe related to Vivi? The young man ran his finger through his hair.

His pinky finger was missing, like Trevor's. What were the odds? The only other person I'd ever seen with a missing pinky was—

Holy. Cow. I suddenly knew why I recognized him. The world spun.

This was Vivi's dad, years ago, Signor Bonacelli, before she was even born, before any of her brothers were born, before he got married. He was barely older than me.

What was he doing here? Why couldn't I have brought Vivi with me this time? Or maybe it was just as well I didn't. Seeing your own parent back in time . . . how weird would that be?

"Why don't you ask him a question?" a woman facing the

opposite bookshelf whispered to me. She turned and winked. It was the palm reader!

"I can't write about Vivi's dad for my history report! I need to see *ancient* Rome!" I hissed at her.

"Today isn't yesterday. There's more than one thing for you to see. Go find out what."

Trembling, I sat in the chair across from him. What if I messed up his future and Vivi was never born? That happened a lot in time travel movies. I didn't have the brains to solve that kind of problem.

This young man in front of me had a lot of heartache in front of him, with the loss of his wife. And a lot of hard work, running his B&B and raising his children at the same time. But he'd have Vivi. So he was lucky.

"Do you need something?" he asked without lifting his head.

I angled my head to get a glimpse of his page. I saw words in stanzas. "You write poetry?"

The shock in my tone probably didn't make sense to anyone else, but this was the guy who scorned artistic pursuits! The one who told Vivi to give up on her dreams!

He flushed a deep brick red, slamming shut his notebook. "No. I do not."

"I just saw it," I pointed out. "It's okay—I write poetry, too."

I do? Well, technically, I had. And I liked it.

The world didn't screech to a halt at the thought.

Vivi's dad—Past Dad—studied me with drawn brows. "What do you write about?"

"Um, well, mostly about Rome so far."

Vivi's dad looked down at his own notebook.

Art requires courage. Michelangelo's words floated through my mind, sinking in like ink on wet paper.

I heard myself saying, "I could . . . show you? One of my poems, I mean."

Lucas, what are you doing? He'll laugh! They always laugh!

He nodded, his face clearing some. With trembling hands, I pulled out my notebook, opened to the last page, where I'd jotted down the short poem about the bookstore. That was silly. Funny. Like me.

But I turned the page further back, to my poem, "Inside/ Outside," about the Pantheon. That one was the most real thing I'd written. It showed my heart.

Sliding my notebook across the table, I fought to not hunch my shoulders as he began reading.

He was going to tell me it was dumb. That I should give up. That I was a joke—I almost reached across the table to snatch the notebook away.

But when he looked up, his smile looked so much like Vivi's that I froze.

He said, "This is very good!"

A new space expanded inside me, giving my lungs more room to breathe. "*Really?*"

"So surprised?"

I pointed him to the limerick. "Funny stuff like that is more my speed, usually."

He read it and chuckled. "Art should also make us laugh! Nothing wrong with that. I write about Rome, too. I'm not funny, though."

I snorted. "Trust me, funny is overrated."

"I also write about other places, places I'd like to see one day."

Well. What did you know? He and his future daughter had a lot more in common than they knew. And actually, I did, too.

I smiled. Sharing art really did take courage. But it was worth it. Michelangelo knew what was up. "Well, I hope you keep writing. And traveling. They work really well together."

Again, I stopped short, surprised by my own words. But they were true. I never would have tried to write a poem like the one I shared without traveling here and living through all this.

He smiled slowly in response. "Thank you . . . and you are?"

Could I tell him?

The coin began to burn in my pocket.

I guess the answer to that question was no.

"I'm a fellow poet! Gotta run, sorry! Just remember—art is worth the effort, even if it's not your day job!"

"Day job?" He sounded confused, but I ran out the front door (couldn't risk giving Vivi's dad a heart attack if I disappeared in front of him) and blinked in the sudden dimness of the bathroom, complete with the *David* statue seat cover.

The doorbell jingled beyond the bathroom. The coin was already cooling off. That was maybe the shortest trip yet. But the most amazing.

In a much better mood, I hurried out of the bookstore and squinted into the bright Roman morning. That visit felt special. Maybe it would help Vivi somehow. She deserved it.

And it was really neat to know that someone as fierce and practical as Signor Bonacelli liked poetry, too.

Inspired, I sent Kei the image of the toilet seat but then took a deep breath. *Courage*, I reminded myself.

I added my favorite shot I'd taken, the one of the *Pietà*. It looked really professional, I thought. Hopefully he'd dig it, too. On impulse, I sent him a dozen more real photos of my last few days. It was time to let others see some of my real work. That's what artists did.

CHAPTER FOURTEEN
A Big Step

Heading over to Vivi and David at the corner, I was dying to tell her who I'd met, but it would have to wait until she and I were alone. The way David was chatting her up would have made me grumpy before. Now I just pictured his face stamped all over a toilet seat and laughed to myself.

The strumming of a guitar echoed down the alley. When I caught up with them, David waved toward the sound, with a giant grin on his stupid face. "Vivi, it's that guy I was telling you about! You've got to hear him play! Maybe even ask him for lessons!"

She shook her head even as her body turned toward the music. "My father would never allow me to take lessons. I've asked. And Lucas doesn't have much time left in Italy—we can't waste a minute."

I took a step toward her. "But you could still show your American friend how street performers play around here, right? That's not wasting anything. I could include it in my journal." I'd seen plenty of street buskers over the months we'd been traveling, but if taking a time-out from my project let her enjoy some music, I was all for it.

She clasped her hands together. "Really?"

"Let's go!" I said. David gave me an almost-smile and a sort of head nod. I mirrored it back, uncertain what it meant, but figured it was better than literally looking down his nose at me.

The strumming of the guitar grew louder as we turned the corner into the sunlit square. A small crowd was already surrounding the source of the sound, but we squirmed our way through it. David got held up just behind us, but Vivi and I got to the front row—one benefit of not being football-player-sized. I tried not to feel gleeful and totally failed.

A bluesy guitar riff exploded from the dude's strings. Vivi gasped. "Oh! Listen to him! He's amazing!"

I didn't know a lot about guitar, but it was clear the guy knew his stuff. Each note flowed right into the next one, smooth and easy. He hunched over the white guitar, connected to an amp, his guitar case open for tips. Plenty of coins had already been tossed in, and I could see why. The man's fingers moved so quickly on the neck of the guitar that they blurred. His eyes weren't even open.

My hand reached for my phone without thinking, and I took the shot, tilting my phone slightly to capture the whole door frame behind him. It made him look almost like one of those sculptures in the alcoves at the Pantheon. Ms. Deblasio would definitely dig this one. It might not be ancient history, but it was Roman through and through.

Cool. I bet I could even write a neat poem about it. I'd do that later tonight, for sure. I patted my pocket, reassured by the weight of my little notebook.

Jeez, I was looking forward to writing poetry. Who was I, even?

A woman in red heels dropped in a bill before leaving. The guitarist sat more upright and switched tunes, something slower but somehow sassy.

"I know this song!" Vivi said. "It's an old folk song, but he's turned it into something jazzy and so much fun!" Her sparkling grin made her prettier than ever. I could tell David obviously noticed the same thing, from the dazed look on his dumb face. He'd finally made his way right behind us.

"You should sing!" The idea burst from me. "Like at the Pantheon!"

She shook her head. "I don't think so."

David called over to the guitarist in a flurry of Italian, ignoring her laughing protests.

The guy nodded at Vivi and gestured her over before flicking his fingers back to the guitar.

"Oh, I couldn't—I shouldn't—"

I thought of her dad, alone in that bookstore, scribbling his poetry and never showing anyone. I whispered to her, "When else will you have such a great chance to try out your dream? Don't be afraid. Art requires courage."

The words seemed to travel right down her spine. She stood up straight and tall and walked—no, *sauntered*—to stand next to the busker. He winked at her—*really, guy?*—and kept playing, glancing up at her just as the music started again with the same refrain.

This time, Vivi sang. It was in Italian, so I didn't know what she was singing, but it didn't matter. Her voice was rich and deeper than it seemed like it should be, coming out of that small frame. Her eyes drifted shut as she matched her voice to the guitar. I brought my phone up and shifted it to video, pressing the record button.

A larger crowd gathered, and I panned the camera around to capture the growing size, all entranced by this girl's voice against the backdrop of soulful guitar.

It lasted maybe a minute and a half, but it felt much longer to me. I wondered if the moment felt stretched out like that to her, too. I'd have to ask her later.

When she finished, everyone applauded and a few people whistled. The guitar player tugged her down to speak to her over the noise. Whatever he said made her blush. She nodded at him, grinning like a maniac.

She practically skipped over to us.

"That. Was. Amazing! Thank you so much, boys!" Her smile was for both of us.

"You sounded fantastic!" I said. "Everyone should be able to hear you!"

"Maybe one day," she replied with a sigh. "But for now, I think it's time we head back, no?" She explained to David, "We've got a trip this afternoon with his family, and then Lucas has a lot to do before he flies out tomorrow."

He lifted his eyebrows. "So soon?"

"We're just visiting."

With his smile, he looked a little too pleased at my answer. On our walk back, we dropped David off at the bookstore. He gave me a hard look before nodding. "Any friend of Viviana's is a friend of mine. If you ever make it back to Rome, I hope to see you around sometime."

"Same here," I lied. "*Ciao*."

I was glad I got a word of Italian in.

On our way back, I didn't waste any time filling in Vivi. "Listen, I've been ready to explode, waiting to tell you. I traveled back in time when we were in the bookstore." My words practically tripped over themselves in their rush to get out.

"How far back did you go?" she asked, clutching my arm.

I swallowed hard, hoping this conversation went smoothly. "I met your father as a young man. Like, way before you were born."

Her hand dropped loosely to her side, and she stopped moving. It was like she was rooted to the ground. "You—you saw . . . my father? Years ago?"

"Yeah. I'll tell you everything." *Just stay calm.* I led her to a nearby bench and helped her sit down. Then I described meeting her younger father, and how he was a poet but seemed embarrassed by it.

"I had no idea that he'd had such an interest." Vivi kept taking long, deep breaths, shaking her head in amazement. She leaned her elbows on her knees, head lowered.

"Hey, are you okay?" I asked. Her eyes were unfocused, but her olive skin still held some pink in the cheeks, so that was a good sign. "It's okay that I told you, right? I wanted to grab you, but I didn't have any time. I didn't know where it was taking me, even."

She blinked rapidly, lifting her gaze to mine. "No, of course, it's fine. Just thinking . . . what if I had been with you?"

I shook my head. "I think that might have been a little too weird. You're not feeling sick, are you? Going to freak out?"

She gave a chuckle that somehow didn't sound happy. "No, but I'm sad he never trusted himself or his poems." Her lips squeezed tight before she said, "I wish I could have read some."

My heart ached. I rubbed at my chest. She caught my worried expression and patted my arm. "Don't worry, Lucas. I can handle it. Thank you for encouraging him to stay true to his dreams. That will always mean so much to me."

Tell her your feelings, Lucas. I took a deep breath. Let it out. I could do this.

"What? You look really anxious." Vivi asked, attention zeroed in on me now, fully focused. "Did something else happen with my father, something you haven't told me?"

The right words wouldn't come.

Strike two.

"No, I was just going to say, you should definitely go for your dreams. Don't give up on them like your dad did."

She studied my face. "And what about you? And your photography?"

I leaned back against the bench and cleared my throat. "Uh, I don't really know what I want to do with my life. It's not the same."

Coward! I was acting just like Vivi's dad, clapping shut that notebook, keeping that part of myself shut away. I didn't want to live like that for the rest of my life, not now that I'd discovered that I really did have things to say.

I gulped. "The thing is . . . I do like photography"—I winced—"and even poetry, but liking something doesn't make you good at it." Michelangelo wouldn't understand. My belly felt tight.

Her brow furrowed, and she gently put a hand on my arm. "Who told you such a terrible thing? Your parents surely would never!"

I shook my head. "Just an offhand comment someone told me once, but it stuck. In third grade, I tried out for the talent show, right?"

"Did you take photos?"

I chuckled. "No, I sang. And I can't hold a tune, so I'm sure it was torture to hear—but when I told my teacher I loved to sing, she informed me that enjoyment was no measure of talent or success. Old Ms. Sala." I kept my tone light, despite the dart of pain.

Vivi's angry frown softened into pure sadness as she sat back. "What a horrible thing to tell a child. Surely she was joking? And you were just too young to understand what was, assuredly, a very bad joke?"

My voice stayed low. "Maybe. But after that, I didn't want to ask her any questions and look dumb, so I fell behind. Then I really *couldn't* do the work. I was never the best in reading, and then science textbooks were getting harder and I couldn't keep up. So I've never really done good in school."

"Oh, Lucas. Lots of kids need help with reading or math . . . those are just learned skills. They have nothing to do with intelligence! You're so smart!"

No need to tell Vivi that Ms. Sala was followed by Ms. Anderson and her frequent lectures on sitting still, and Mr. Carter's gentle but frustrating warnings about not meeting my potential. Too humiliating. I couldn't do anything about the past, anyway. Even though I'd had lots of cool teachers after those few rough years who offered to help me, it felt too late. My grades went downhill from there.

Vivi leaned into me a little. She radiated as much warmth as the sun. "I think you'll figure it out."

"What, school or my career?"

"Both. Either."

"I'm glad one of us is confident."

She grinned up at me with the smile that I was coming to realize was totally Vivi—mischievous and fun-filled. I began to worry less about her dad keeping her trapped behind the counter of their gelato shop. This girl was both sweet and surprisingly sassy. It was part of her charm.

She said, "Tell you what—you believe in me and I'll believe in you. And we'll do what we can to help the other become real artists."

This was too intense. I should play it cool, pull back, crack a joke . . . but instead, I held out my hand. "Okay. Deal." She shook it once, nice and strong.

I had an idea. "Hey, what if we upload your singing video online? Right now, today?"

She frowned. "Oh, but my father—"

"Wouldn't have to know! Or if he did, maybe he'd finally realize how good you are!" I tried to tone down my voice, but I was so excited, it was hard to stay chill.

She chewed her lip. "I don't know, Lucas."

I wanted to help her take this step. So I would take a big one of my own. "How about this? You post this, and I'll send my photos into a national competition. You can help me find one. That way, we're really helping each other follow our dreams, right?"

Her smile was like the sun coming out from behind the clouds. "Let's do it!"

We hunched over my phone and worked our way through the uploading process. My stomach was full of butterflies armed with steel swords or something.

The hits started almost right away. Five. Ten. Thirty.

Her squeal made me laugh, and we danced around like fools right there in the street. But we really did have to go, so we ran home, hope sending us flying.

By the time we got back to the shop, there was barely time for a quick lunch—I'd have to write my notes later—and then my parents and brothers joined us for the walk to Piazza Navona.

Robby rambled about the history of the piazza. Apparently, he'd taken advantage of his time home this morning to memorize everything online about it. Jeez, who needed a trip back in time when you had this guy around?

"And during the Olympics . . ." he continued to fill us in with deets I was hoping to get in person. "But then later . . ."

A piazza in Italy was what we in the States would call a town square. Piazza Navona was really more like a long, narrow rectangle, thanks to the small stadium it had been built on, with three big fountains dotted down the middle.

I turned to my parents. "We were here on the first day, right? It was drizzling, though, so the artists weren't here then."

"Hmmm, yes," Mom said with narrowed eyes. "As I recall, you sat over there on that bench and ate French fries. And played on your phone. And took not one picture."

Vivi swatted my arm. "Seriously, Lucas?"

I winced, and not from the swat. "I was tired that day."

I'd been tired almost every day of our trip, it seemed. Until lately. Today my feet felt light and springy, ready for an adventure.

Happily, there was nothing but sunshine now. Easels stood up and down the open courtyard. Travelers weighed down with backpacks sat around the edges of the fountains. In the center of the fountain, a sculpture of a huge sea serpent seemed to be losing a battle with what might be Neptune. But maybe it was Oceanus. I really should figure out how to tell them apart.

My parents and brothers nerded out right away, as they do,

oohing and aahing over the fact that this square used to host footraces and how the Tiber flooded so often that the dirt just built up over time like sixteen feet higher. There was really ancient stuff under the ground, and the cobblestoned square we were standing on was *already* old. That was pretty crazy amazing.

Soon, my parents headed over to one of the shops to talk to the owner about whatever their interview had been about. I guess I could have asked. Maybe it would have been good for my report.

And, really, it would just be kinda cool to know.

Trevor pointed out the artists. "Can we get a painting?"

I shook my head. "Out of our budget, little man. But maybe you can draw us a picture of this later, huh? So look at everything really carefully."

"I wanna see the big fountain in the middle!" he declared.

We moved to the center fountain, and Robby talked to us about how each statue dude in the fountain represented a different river and part of the world.

I pulled out my phone to take a few shots of the sculptures that rose above the basin—totally serious photos—but nothing happened. Worry began to simmer inside me. I needed to travel in time. But the coin sat still and cold. I even got down on my belly to take a picture using a steep upward angle, like I'd chickened out of at the Colosseum.

Nothing.

As I stood and dusted myself off with a huff, Vivi pursed her lips and said, "Maybe you need a new angle."

"I just tried that, though," I said, irritated that I'd embarrassed myself on the ground for nothing. Though I really hadn't gotten nearly as many stares as I thought I would.

"I mean, maybe you're not focusing on what you're supposed to, silly!" She mimed holding a camera up to her eye, looking around the square through it with exaggerated delight.

It was impossible not to smile. I didn't remind her that my last shot prior to time traveling had been one of her, but maybe she had a point. It was time to expand my focus.

CHAPTER FIFTEEN

Then and Now

Vivi pointed behind me with a smile. "For example: look at that lady over there with her dog. Isn't that sweet?"

An old woman sat on a bench offering the last of her ice-cream cone to her shaggy brown dog. The pup happily gobbled the treat, and she scolded the dog in Italian.

"What's she saying?" I wondered aloud.

"That he should not be such a slob." Vivi giggled.

We watched together as the old woman leaned down with a napkin and wiped the dog's furry mouth. I could really see how much she loved that dumb dog. Vivi was right. It was sweet. And I didn't use that word lightly.

I raised my phone and took the photo and double-checked.

Wow. It actually was . . . adorable. Authentic. You could feel the woman's affection across the screen, and messy Gelato Dog was super cute.

It was a dang awesome photo, even without any famous landmarks, maybe because it was a dang awesome moment, in real life.

A goofy grin split my face. I couldn't stop it.

My brothers would want to see Gelato Dog, too—Trevor

was a huge fan of all things canine. I turned to where they sat on the edge of the fountain. As I watched, Trevor leaned way over the water, but before I could even warn him about falling in, Robby whispered in his ear and Trevor slid back to the safe zone. Robby glanced my way, and I gave him a thumbs-up.

Their two faces turned upward to study the giant stone statue, profiled against the ancient buildings behind them. Inspired, I lifted my phone, took a shot while holding my breath . . . and smiled at the result.

Here was another real-life moment: a picture of the fountain *with* my brothers—this image captured our afternoon more fully than the statue alone. Family. Family was home, isn't that was Signora Russo had said?

Robby's face from last night popped in my mind, when he was so worried about being left behind and so delighted at being included. I remembered how Trevor held on to my waist when he was tired and trusted me to take care of him. The way we all fought a lot—but always made up. We were family.

The coin began to heat in my pocket.

"Hey! Vivi! Quick, it's happening!" *Ancient Olympics, here we come!*

She grabbed hold of my hand, standing so close I could feel her warmth. Brightness blinded me, and when I opened my eyes . . .

Everything looked almost exactly the same.

Tourists in jeans, in shorts, holding selfie sticks, speaking in a dozen languages. The only difference was the square was less crowded and the sun was hidden behind gray clouds.

"What?" Vivi said. "Why is it cloudy all of a sudden?"

It began to rain.

My breath came fast. "I don't know."

Vivi examined the people around us with narrowed eyes.

"What's this?" I said. "I'm not going to learn anything for my project with another short hop to modern times!" A stab of panic sent ice through me. "I need a live-action *historical* replay to write about!"

The tattooed palm reader walked around the fountain. "Or perhaps you *need* something else."

"What's going on?" I demanded, my voice cracking like a gunshot. Because this moment wasn't disconcerting enough.

She grinned at me. "You've got feisty brothers. It must run in the family." She grabbed my hand and studied my palm. "Hmm. It looks like you need to reconnect with something important."

She was really weird. And annoying.

I glared at her and said, "This place was supposed to show us the ancient Olympic Games."

The palm reader replied, "There are all kinds of games being played today. You'll see. But be extra cautious who you choose to speak to here. Being too *self-aware* would be a very bad thing. Dangerous, even."

Dangerous?

Luckily, self-awareness really wasn't my strength. Just then

I heard my mother's voice. "Lucas, did you see this great statue by Bernini? I think it represents the River Nile."

I turned to answer that I actually knew that, thanks to Robby's lecture, but a familiar voice replied before I could. "Yeah, Mom. It's cool."

My words floated out of my head like helium balloons.

Moving slowly, I peered around the side of the center fountain. A dark-haired boy with a big nose sat on a bench, slumping under an umbrella. His eyes were glued to his phone screen. And he wasn't evaluating photos or reading up on the piazza.

I knew, because I remembered this moment exactly. It was from two weeks ago, the last time I was here.

Chills ran up and down my body, and I sucked in a long breath.

One hand at her throat, Vivi said, "Is that—"

"Me? Uh, yeah, it is."

"Oh my gosh, get down!" Vivi hissed, yanking me to the ground by the edge of my shirt, hiding behind the giant fountain. "Your family is here, your family from the past!"

Vivi's other hand clamped on her own mouth. Her muffled words came through as a squeak, "And the magic lady just disappeared."

Of course she had.

Rain dripped down my face, and I wiped it off. My mother— my then-mother, in her crisp rain jacket with a hood—walked over to Past Lucas. Her voice echoed across the piazza to where I stood directly opposite from them both. "Are you just going to sit there, honey? You know you need to document all this for class."

"Yeah, I get it. It's just like every other fountain we've seen, though." The old me barely glanced up.

Rude. Shame flooded me. I wanted to glance to check Vivi's reaction but kept my gaze locked forward on my mother.

My mom turned away for a minute, and I got a clear look of frustration on her face—no, wait. Hurt. She was hurt.

A golf ball formed in my throat.

My then-mother said, "Fine." Her words were short and sharp. She didn't *sound* hurt, but I knew what I'd seen. "But if you have any questions, I'm here for you. Dad, too. We brought you with us so we could share this amazing history together. I wish—"

Past-me shrugged.

I kinda wanted to punch him. Me.

Mom was still talking to the statue that was her son. "Well, it's just two more weeks of this trip. You'll survive, I'm sure. Keep an eye on your brothers, please. Dad and I are going to go be around the corner at the café, doing an interview. Get us if there are any problems."

Past-me barely grunted agreement, at least looking up long enough to eyeball our brothers' location before returning to the game.

My mother stepped around puddles to reach my dad at the far end of the piazza. My hiding spot wasn't much of a hiding spot from that angle.

I slid backward to join Vivi behind a clump of determined tourists in rain jackets.

Dad's deeper voice carried his words. "Any response?"

Mom shook her head. "None. I just want to share the dream of my life with *all* our children. Is that so wrong?"

He kissed her cheek. "Of course not."

Of course not. I wanted to tell her so myself, but of course I couldn't.

She gave a deep sigh. "The thing is, I think he'd love Rome if he gave it a chance. He's got such *potential.*"

I winced. I hated that word, had heard it all my life . . . but my mom's sadness made me feel smaller than that word ever had.

"Oh Lucas," Vivi whispered, her voice rich with sympathy.

Better sympathy than disgust. Now she'd seen the horrible, ugly truth. We both had. I wasn't failing just because I wasn't super smart. I wasn't even *trying,* despite my parents spoon-feeding me awesomeness. Or I hadn't been trying, until the last few days.

I shook my head. "I guess I wanted people to think I could do a good job if I *wanted* to. Instead of being disappointed when I really couldn't."

"But how do you know you can't?" She lifted one eyebrow. "It's been many years since you've stopped trying, it sounds like."

She had a point. "I think I stopped trying and just made people laugh instead because . . ."

"Because if you don't try, you won't get hurt."

I nodded. Hopefully it wasn't too late to start trying for real.

My parents left the piazza, which at least meant two fewer

people who could potentially lose their mind if they saw us back here.

"Now what?" Vivi said. "You always seem to talk to someone from the past before you return . . . but I don't think you should talk to yourself!"

"I don't know."

Vivi tapped her lip. "Well, what was the last image you took before we came back here?"

I swiped through the other shots of the day. "The coin took us back right after I took a shot of my brothers . . ." I held out my phone, flipped to the image, and studied it.

I remembered that swamping feeling of brotherly love that struck after I'd taken it.

"That's it!" I breathed. "The shot that triggers a trip through time has to capture something important—to me. Like feeling connected to my brothers." Even the toilet seat was something that made me feel connected to Kei, because we always shared stupid photos.

The realization was like a click in a lock tumbler, setting free a cascade of understanding. So few of my photos of our journey had anyone in them. No friends or family. These past six months had been a lonely time, despite my family, and my photos certainly captured that. But now? I had a friend here. I had a family. And they just wanted to share life with me. They always had.

A young voice spoke behind us, one I knew. "Lucas? Why

aren't you under the umbrella?" I turned, and Trevor stood there, wet and glowing with delight. And he was coated with mud—ugh.

But wait. *No.* I sucked in a long breath and heard Vivi doing the same.

This was Trevor from two weeks ago. When he'd gotten in trouble for rolling in the mud. And I'd gotten in trouble for not watching him closely enough.

"Um." *Trevor from the past saw me. He saw me.* My heart raced. *Dangerous.* The word came back to haunt me. *Dangerous.*

I had to get him away from us. Well, I had a message I wanted to send, for real. Why not try it? "Hey, Trevor, can you go tell Mom that I really do want to know more about that fountain? Just tell her that for me? She just went around the corner."

His face puckered. "You're not my boss. Why don't you tell her that yourself?"

He stomped off, and I gave a deep sigh. He asked an excellent question.

Trevor was so in his own little world that he never noticed I was in a different T-shirt. Small blessings. But no way was he going to pass on that message.

I guess I'd have to tell her. Myself.

The coin got hot.

"Hurry! The coin!" Gasping, I flung my hand out to Vivi, who grabbed it and pressed herself to my side. A steady fire grew along the side of my leg where the coin rested.

The flash left us blinking, as always. "Wow," I said. "Seeing *myself* back in time was . . . wow. Unexpected." The coin felt riskier now. I might not read a lot, but even I knew that messing with your own timeline could really screw up the future. Plenty of movies covered that topic.

"That was astonishing!" Vivi crowed. "Honestly, now I'm glad the coin didn't bring me with you at the bookstore. I think I would have fainted, flat onto the floor! I wonder if Signora saw her own parents, too!" Her eyes glowed, her hair swirled . . . prettier than ever.

It was the perfect moment for a snapshot. Questions of time travel were important, and so was passing my class, but I didn't want to miss my chance again.

"Hold that thought and say cheese," I told Vivi and lifted my phone like I'd wanted to since that moment at the Colosseum.

I took her picture with the fountain splashing behind her, with the obelisk rising high from the center and her face full of joy and fun.

"Let me see!" She turned my phone around and nodded. "You really could be a photographer one day, Lucas. That might be the nicest photo of me ever taken." Her eyes crinkled just a little at the corners when she smiled.

My heart was racing, although maybe it was just from the shock of seeing myself in the past.

"How about a selfie with both of us?" she asked. It seemed to worry her exactly zero percent to ask. Confidence looked good on her. My heart sped faster—and it definitely wasn't related to the coin. Not this time.

I held out the phone for the picture, turning us so the

fountain was behind us in all its glory. Her curls filled up half the screen. She pulled them back with a laugh to make more space.

Then her face suddenly straightened, and she said in her most formal voice, "Shall we point to their rears? Perhaps pick their noses?" she deadpanned, gesturing to the statues. "For your Kei?"

Laughter competed with embarrassment. "How about we just smile like normal people?"

"Oh, you want us to pretend? Okay then." Her grin was infectious. "*Sorridi!*" she said. The R's rolled like curly ribbons on a present. The Italian language made everything sound fancy.

"What's that mean?" I lowered my phone for a moment.

"It's like your version of 'Say cheese!'"

"Oh! Then *sorridi!*" I said and took the shot, both of us smiling like loons. A swirl of giddiness rushed through me. I felt so happy, I wanted to share it. It was too much to hold inside.

My brothers were now sitting on one of the benches, shoulders slumped.

"I can't believe Mom and Dad aren't back yet," Robby said, sounding totally bummed out even though he was sitting in the sunshine in Rome. "The Olympics museum is just over there. We're going to run out of time if they don't hurry up!"

"I know," I said, "but we'll do what we can to have fun while we wait."

Pulling my brothers up from the bench, I led us to one of the artists to watch him work. Robby, in particular, had a good eye for art. The artist generously explained his process and posed for a few shots of him with my brothers. I bet they'd both remember this moment with a smile. I knew I would.

Finally, Mom and Dad hurried around the corner—today's Mom and Dad, thankfully. "Hey, kids! Ready for the museum about the old stadium that used to be here? We thought it might be good for the book. Want to join us?"

Without hesitation, I reached a hand to my brothers, "Let's see if we can make the past come alive, what do you say?"

Vivi winked at me.

Robby took my hand and grabbed Trevor's, who grabbed Vivi's, so my brothers were sandwiched between us. Robby said, "Let's go. I already studied up on it."

"I'm sure you did," I said with a smile. "Hey, Mom," I called as we headed out. "Wasn't that statue in the middle supposed to be the Nile or something?"

Her eyes lit up, and she started talking. This time, I listened.

And the museum?

It was actually really cool. I didn't even take notes—I just listened and paid close attention, like a sponge. It was a new sensation for me. I liked it.

CHAPTER SIXTEEN
A New Focus

"So, you've gotten dozens of fabulous photographs," Vivi said a couple hours later as we walked back to the B&B. "Do you think that's enough?"

"I don't know. I wish I'd have gone farther back in time . . . but I'm also glad I didn't." That trip felt . . . more important than all the others, somehow.

I'd gotten several more pictures of my brothers, but that wasn't all. I got one of a bird landing on an artist's easel, bunches of roses at a flower stand, and a close-up of the sunlight bouncing off the water in the fountain.

I also took a few more of Vivi, sometimes laughing, sometimes thinking, but always enjoying the moment. She made it impossible for me not to do the same. I wish we would have gone sightseeing together when I first got here. Now we'd just have to say goodbye tomorrow.

My parents showed up in some of my shots finally, too. It might have been the first time I'd intentionally tried to get them in a picture. By the time we were ready to head back to the B&B for the night, our stomachs were growling.

"We did good today?" Trevor asked, hopefully. "Pizza for dinner?"

My dad adjusted his glasses. "Sounds great! Vivi, you're welcome to join us."

Trevor wrapped his arms around Vivi's waist. "Please?"

She hugged him tightly, the lucky kid. "I wish I could, but I'll need to get some work done tonight. But I'm so thankful for this time with you today." She spoke to my whole family, but it seemed she had a special smile just for me. Maybe. I hoped so.

We set off toward the B&B. I walked next to Vivi, with my brothers paired up in front of us, and my parents behind us. The bustle of the crowd was louder now than it had been this morning.

I spoke to Vivi without looking at her. "Will we see you in the morning before we go?" I bit back the words that crowded my mouth: *I'll miss you, Vivi.*

"I wouldn't miss saying goodbye." Her voice was soft.

I wished we could hang out tonight—it was our last chance. But even if she were free, I wasn't.

My stomach twisted a little with nerves. I still had to write all of today's entries, plus type up everything from the last three weeks (really shouldn't have procrastinated on that) and submit it by midnight. Like I told Vivi, reaching for an A hadn't been my style—why shoot for the stars when you can't even get off the launchpad?—but I definitely had a good chance to make it this time if I worked hard tonight.

That hope felt like driving through the wide-open plains

after winding through confusing mountain roads. It would work out. It had to. And if I did end up taking summer school, maybe I'd manage to talk my way into tryouts despite missing soccer camp. There were always exceptions.

Before dinner, alone in my bedroom, I listened to Vivi singing again on my phone and watched the likes on the video climb for the next hour. One thousand. Two thousand. Three thousand. And I hardly had any followers, so this was freaking amazing. I wanted to celebrate with her again, but I didn't have her number. I clicked on my contacts . . . and my jaw dropped.

Viviana Bonacelli. It was right there. And her number! She'd put her number in my phone at some point.

My stomach did a big somersault. I felt like I could jump over a skyscraper.

With fingers trembling only a little, I tapped out a message.

Hey, it's Lucas. When did you have my phone? I see your number in it.

Three tiny dots flashed at me almost right away.

Her response appeared in under thirty seconds.

When you were checking out at the bookstore. I took it out of your pocket. Are you angry?

If she could see my grin, she wouldn't need to ask.

Don't be silly. Now I have the number of a famous musician! I sent the link to the video.

A long pause. Then:

OH MY GOSH! LUCAS! THIS IS AMAZING!

You sound great, right? Didn't I say so?

She sent a blushing emoji.

I replied: Almost 4000 likes already!

She responded, Thank you for cheering me on.

Without thinking twice, I wrote back: Always, V.

I meant it, too. I'd always be there for Vivi.

I started working on my project for the night, flipping through my photos. I kinda regretted sending the *Pietà* picture and the others to Kei now that the moment had passed—serious stuff just wasn't how we functioned, the two of us—but . . . well, too late now. Besides, I was proud of it.

I was really proud of my poem about the Piazza Navona, too. I hoped my English teacher liked it. Mr. Franklin might pull a Ms. Sala on me, but I wouldn't let him get me down. I liked it. Shoot, maybe I'd even show that to Kei, too.

Thinking of Kei, I checked the time and decided to give him a quick call.

When he answered, I grinned. "Hey horseface!"

He did not grin back. "Well, well, well. It's Mr. Italy. How's it going?" His words sounded sharp, and his face stayed stony. That wasn't like him at all.

It suddenly felt too warm in the room. "Um, could be worse, I guess?"

He smiled, but it had a weird edge to it like he'd just pulled a muscle or something. "Looks like you're finally getting all into your trip, just before you come home."

Discomfort had me shifting in my seat. It felt like I'd walked onstage and was in the wrong play. All the lines were wrong. "Could be. Sooo, what did you think of the . . . pictures?" I didn't want to ask, but I couldn't not. He was just acting too weird. I had a bad feeling about this.

Kei popped his gum and shrugged. "They're okay. But they aren't really your style, are they?"

"My style?" My pulse began to thud in my ears.

He flapped a hand in the air. "Yeah, you're taking things too seriously, man! The *David* toilet seat, that was genius, but the rest? The old buildings and stuff? The sad lady holding the dead guy? What's that about?"

"Um, that was Jesus?" I could feel my eyes popping. I struggled to hold on to my chill.

"Whatever dude. It was *dark*. Since when do you like stuff that's all serious and boring? It's obviously messing with your brain, man. Relax!"

I shook my head. "But—"

He gave a gusty sigh and leaned back like he was about to deliver another movie lecture, rating how good it was. Except this time, he was scoring my life. "But nothing. I know you, okay? You're not that guy, the emo-dude in the little beanie, sipping coffee. The team next year? They'll never let you live it down if you show back up here acting like that. Next thing you know, you'll start going to poetry slams or something."

His words were a punch to the gut. Was he right? My mind flashed back to Vivi's dad. And then to my own poems.

"Would it be so bad if I did? Start liking poetry, I mean?"

It was true, our soccer team wasn't known for its collective GPA, but the others kept solid Bs and Cs. Why would they care if I suddenly started doing better? If I actually started trying?

He sat up straighter, crossing his arms. "I know living in Europe probably changed some stuff. But you're about to be back here with the rest of us jerks, so better get used to your old life. We aren't so fancy as your girl there."

Anger bubbled up, making it easy to shove the hurt aside. "Don't talk about Vivi. She's awesome!"

He snorted. "Yeah, that's what I thought this was about. I get it, okay? She's pretty. But girls like that don't go for funny guys. They go for leading-man types, the serious guys. And that's not you, man."

I pulled in a long breath. My expression must have been fierce because he rolled his eyes. "Jeez, don't get all sensitive on me. I didn't mean—"

"No, I think you did. I'm cool as long as I'm just a big joke, is that it?"

He's right. Who do you think you are?

Kei winced. "No, that's not what I meant."

"Then what did you mean?" I crossed my own arms and waited.

He shrugged, staring off to the side of the screen. "Nothing, man. Just forget I said anything."

Not likely. A cold lump sat in my belly. "Whatever. I'd better go. I still have a project to finish. So I can pass my classes. Because I'm seriously one grade away from failing eighth grade completely, so thanks for the support, man."

He opened his mouth, finally looking at me, blinking with shock, but I clicked to hang up.

I shouldn't have even told him how bad my grades were. I didn't want to hear his pity.

You're not that guy . . .

His words kept echoing in my mind.

I'd thought sharing about the local Rome I saw today was going to be really cool. I'd written down a lot of information in the bookstore, especially. But now I felt sick to my stomach. That new open space inside me collapsed into a cold, hard knot. If I were the Pantheon, the dome just fell in.

Maybe my new work wasn't nearly as good as I thought. Kei sure hadn't seemed impressed with it. Maybe after all this work, I was going to fail anyway.

And then *everyone* would know the truth: my best just wasn't enough.

Unable to face the blank page, I checked my upload of Vivi's singing. Wow, it had over ten thousand likes already! That was *huge*. Better than I'd ever dreamed. It was really happening—she was going viral! The painful knot loosened a bit in my chest.

If I was going to fail after all, at least one of us would live our dream.

Of course, if she heard me say that, she'd say, *You deserve happiness, too. You can do this.*

A memory of Michelangelo's gruff voice joined in: *I will not crawl when I can walk, no matter how my body aches.*

I had to do this. Somehow, I had to write. I reached for my notebook. At least I had my notes. . . . I'd start with my basic descriptions of stuff, see what they inspired.

"Here we go!" I into my back pocket and pulled out . . . *A Wrinkle in Time* from Vivi.

Wait. What?

I checked my pockets again. They were empty except for my phone and the coin. No notebook.

A cold sweat broke over me. I guess I thought the rectangular shape in my pocket was my notebook all this afternoon. With the excitement of the time travel trip, I'd actually forgotten about the novel in my pocket.

And now my notebook was gone. It must have fallen out somewhere along the way. I shouldn't have tried to stuff it next to the book.

My brain flickered through all my steps today, trying to figure out where it could be, and then I realized the truth. All of my handwritten notes of my days, my poems, were long gone.

I'd left the notebook back in time with Vivi's dad.

CHAPTER SEVENTEEN

Game Over, Man. Game Over.

How could I have been so *stupid?* I'd been so worried about freaking out Vivi's dad that I'd just taken off when I felt the coin heat up. He'd still been holding the notebook.

Lightning struck just outside the building, making the lights flicker, and the resulting boom shook the walls. The floor trembled under my feet, but I barely noticed. I was trembling already.

My notebook is gone. My notebook is gone. My notebook is gone—

Boom! Thunder exploded again just as someone knocked on the door—loudly.

Maybe it was Vivi, scared by the storm. Or—maybe she'd found the notebook!

That had to be it! She must have picked it up at some point and was going to save me yet again by giving it back right now. "I'll get it!" I called, energy racing through my wobbly legs.

The lights flickered again.

I swung open the door. "Viv—"

Vivi's father stood in the hallway, phone clutched in his hand. For a moment, I saw the younger Mr. Bonacelli superimposed over the elder version, but the memory of earnest eyes quickly faded into some very, very angry ones. He shook the phone at me. "Did you do this?"

Mr. Bonacelli's words were not loud. In fact, they were barely above a whisper, and I'd never been so scared in all my life.

My head swam. "Do what?" But I knew.

He saw the video.

"Did you put my daughter online for the world to see?" His voice remained at a hiss, but his glare could have peeled the paint off the walls if the paint wasn't already peeling.

"I can explain!" I held my palms out, pleading. "She's so good, Mr. Bonacelli, Signor Bonacelli, I mean. And I think that—"

He cut me off with a slice of his hand. This time, his voice kicked up a notch or two. "*You* think? You are just a tourist, here today and gone tomorrow! I've worked hard to convince her to work with our family in a good, steady job, and here you are, getting her hopes up about a silly dream of rock-and-roll stardom."

He sneered those last words. Was the hallway stretching out behind him like a horror movie, or was that just my panic talking? The cold, hard knot from Kei's words returned to my chest with a vengeance.

Crossing my fingers and hoping the coin had life-saving magic, too, I said, "You once wrote poetry from your heart,

Mr. Bonacelli. You gave up on your dreams, I guess, but do you really want that for Vivi?"

He took a step back, shock scribbled across his face. "*What did you say?*"

My mouth was dry, but I spoke quickly. "You used to go sit in Vivi's favorite bookstore—it was yours before hers—and you'd write poetry and dream of travel. The, uh, owner told us today. What happened?"

His Adam's apple bobbed like a cork.

My dad came around the corner. "What's going on? Oh, hello Signor Bonacelli. Can I help you?" His pleasant expression drifted to concern as he glanced between us. "Lucas?"

I blinked hard. "It's fine, Dad. I made a mistake, but I'm going to fix it."

My dad was suddenly at my side, standing straighter than usual. "Does this need to involve me?"

Mr. Bonacelli shook his head slowly like he was waking from a dream. "No, we're fine here." Then he eyeballed me. "Please take Vivi's video offline. Now. And do not visit with her again."

My father frowned. "Now, sir, I'm sure there's been a misunderstanding. My son is a good boy, with strong character. I couldn't be prouder of him."

My dad dropped his hand on my shoulder and squeezed. Just that one little touch. But the weight of that hand felt like it would keep me from flying off into space. My dad's words seeped into me, coating the horror of the moment with a strange sweetness.

I couldn't be prouder of him.

Tears stung my eyes, and I cleared my throat.

Vivi's dad raised his eyebrows. "That is good to know, Mr. Duran. And I agree. I believe our children made some poor choices regarding social media, but nothing that cannot be corrected. Yes?" Vivi's dad asked me.

I nodded so hard my hair flopped into my face. "Yes, sir. I will." Sweat gathered under my arms. Wait, was he blaming Vivi, too? It had been my idea. I should tell him that I totally talked her into it. "It was—"

Another clap of thunder rolled through the room. A few fat drops of rain splattered on the windows. Shadows danced across Mr. Bonacelli's face, and I swear he looked like the devil ready to eat my soul for dessert. My voice died away.

"Then I believe I will take my leave," said the scary devil version of Vivi's dad. He looked to my father. "And will you be staying past tomorrow? We will need to move your room if you do."

So suddenly we were having a normal conversation? My heart still sped like a robber escaping a crime. My dad patted my back, a secret signal telling me it was going to be okay.

"No, Lucas is turning in his final project tonight," he said cheerily, "and we'll be good to go by noon tomorrow. Right, Lucas?" My father squeezed my shoulder again.

I glanced up and saw a question in his eyes. Was I really going to be okay?

Tears threatened to leak from my eyes, but I swallowed them back and nodded, patting his hand with my own.

Mr. Bonacelli said, "Then I'll let you get back to your work." He met my gaze, but there was no comfort in his face. None. There was an echo of something else, though. Fear? Shock? Uncertainty? I'd rattled him with the poem line. Good.

The door closed quietly. "Thanks, Dad."

He pushed his glasses more firmly onto his nose. "I've got your back. Your mom, too. I hope you know that."

I hadn't known that, but I was finally beginning to realize it. The cold, hard spot in my heart had begun to thaw.

My dad broke our silence. "Hey, I'll get some dinner for us. You need brain food if you're going to write a solid last essay."

"Dad, oh my gosh!" The horror of losing my notebook came roaring back. "I lost my notebook today! The one with all my notes. I think it got left behind in the bookstore."

His shoulders slumped. "Which I guess is closed now?"

I nodded. That notebook was long gone, years ago.

"Did it have everything from Rome in it you'd done so far?"

"Yeah. I thought I'd type it all in tonight, but—" I slapped my forehead. "I messed up. As usual. Now, I'll fail for sure."

"You aren't going to fail, Lucas."

"Easy for you to say," I muttered.

If this happened to him, my dad would manage to come up with some wise, insightful stuff off the cuff. All I could effectively pull off on short notice was jokes and basic descriptions. That wouldn't cut it.

My dad rubbed his eyes behind his glasses. "First things first. I'm going to get us some food. Then we'll deal with it! Together."

He grabbed his keys and headed out, so I threw myself on my bed, pulled out my phone, and took down the video. What a waste. I sent her a text.

The video's down now. I'm really sorry!!! Tell him it was all my idea. Also, do you have my notebook? It's missing!

She wrote back within a minute.

Oh no! I don't have it. I'm so sorry! And it's okay about the video. It was amazing while it lasted. How's your project going?

Bad, without the notebook. And Kei basically told me I was full of myself for even trying.

That doesn't sound like him. Something must be wrong.

She had a point.

My family didn't talk about things head-on. Vivi looked small and delicate and sweet, but she was a bull charging forward, fearlessly. My family was more like horses, shying away from any hint of conflict.

She wrote again.

Whoops, Dad's taking my phone now . . . bye!

I felt empty. The thunder had faded completely, and now there was just a steady rain.

My dad burst through the door, holding a pizza box and dripping water everywhere.

"Pizza!" Trevor hollered.

"A pizza margherita made in Italy, the best pizza ever," my dad corrected. He flipped open the lid, and the tangy scent of tomato sauce wafted out. "Crispy thin crust, fresh mozzarella, sweet basil. Last night for it."

I snagged a slice—okay, two—and then hunkered down at the far corner of the table, staring out the window. The steady streaks of rain turned Rome into a watercolor painting, softer and gentler than I'd seen it yet.

Upstairs, Vivi might be looking out at the rain, too, grounded for life, probably, all because of me. Maybe her eyes were even full of tears, blurring the inside of her room like the rain blurred the outside.

The pizza was salty and delicious, but it kept getting stuck in my throat. My confidence was just gone. Zapped. Zilch. I ruined everything. Why not my project, too?

Five hours left. Shoot, I'd just go to bed early and wait for my project's midnight deadline to pass and make my title official: LUCAS DURAN IS THE BIGGEST LOSER IN THE WORLD.

"What's wrong with you?" Robby asked, nose wrinkled. "You've barely eaten one slice."

"Well, let's see." I ticked things off on fingers. "I ruined Vivi's life. Kei got all weird on me. And I'm going to fail my assignment." A bitter taste filled my mouth.

Mom said, "But I've seen you working on it. Your photos are great. You can reconstruct your essays."

I burst out, "I don't remember stuff like you guys, do, okay? I need all my notes! And my other entries were only good because Robby told me all kinds of cool stuff that I included. I don't know enough on my own." *Because I'm the dumb one.*

Robby said, "You don't need anyone's help."

"You're just saying that because you're my brother." I slumped deeper in my seat, heaviness pulling me down.

He slapped his forehead. "Since when does being brothers mean saying nice things about each other? Listen, you've got this. Stop feeling sorry for yourself and start writing."

But I couldn't.

Tiredness mixed with desperation helped set the words free. "But what if I really do fail this year?" I looked at my parents. "Won't I be an embarrassment to y'all with your professor friends?"

My mom furrowed her brow, hand flying to her neck. "Of course not!"

Dad shook his head, confusion in his eyes.

I set down my pizza and glanced at my dad. "So . . . did you mean it earlier, with Vivi's father? That . . . you're proud of me?"

Dad knelt beside me, eye to eye. "I wouldn't have said it if I didn't mean it." He squeezed my shoulder. "Lucas. *Lucas*. I don't care two beans about what my professor friends think. Sure, we want you to pass. But you are kind, and fair, and funny, and generous."

"But—" I began.

"Wait." He lifted his pointer finger. "Hear this. The classroom doesn't always match well with all types of learners—Einstein dropped out of school at fifteen, you know. Grades aren't the only measure of a man. You've got many strengths, and we have no doubt you're going to be very successful in life. Even if you have to go to summer school. It's not the end of the world."

"But I want to pass." I sniffed. My nose was running.

"We know." My dad wrapped me in a hug. My mom joined in. Then my brothers, like one big bear hug.

Surrounded by family like that, I was able to admit some stuff. "I'm scared. I want to graduate with my friends. I want to be on the soccer team." My voice was squeezed off by the tightness in my throat.

My mom held on tight. "Then you'll graduate. You can do all that. You just need to dig deep for this project, and everything you've experienced is already inside you. You've got this."

My lungs kept taking deep breaths until I felt dizzy. I wanted to believe them so badly. But I'd spent years believing I didn't have anything to offer other than soccer goals and jokes.

I hugged them all back—the first in a long time—and smiled over at my mom. That cold, knotted spot in my chest softened a little more.

"You've taught me a lot," Robby said, voice muffled in my shoulder.

"What?" I pulled back.

He quirked a smile. "You don't always show it, but you see things in a really cool way. You taught me a lot yesterday. And I figured out a way I can help—see, I keep a list of everything we've seen and done. You can use it to help remind yourself of everything you need to cover in your essays. In your own words, of course."

The knot dissolved into warmth, opening back up that new-found space inside me. Some fear still lingered, but now it wasn't paralyzing. "Thanks, buddy," I said.

"You're the best, Lucas!" was all Trevor had to say, but it made me smile.

I ruffled his hair. "Thanks, all of you. Really."

Kei was wrong. My pictures, and even my poems, weren't about pretending to be what I wasn't. They were showing who I really was, from my heart. I straightened my back.

My dad patted my shoulder as they left. I checked the time and spread out my brother's list. Four hours until my deadline.

I could do this.

I would.

My fingers hovered over the keyboard, and I chewed my lip. I'd reconstruct the other entries, but first, what to say about today? That I almost told a girl I really liked her but got chewed out by her dad instead? That my best friend thought I was an academic snob when I was barely passing my classes? No, that wasn't what my teachers wanted. They wanted history.

And what stunk was that I *had* written about history. I'd poured my heart out in that journal.

The loss of my notes stung, not just because I wanted them for my project. I wanted them for me, to remember my time here, especially my time with Vivi. I was *proud* of my work.

I'd changed a lot since I first came to Rome.

Or maybe I hadn't changed as much as I'd . . . learned to be honest with myself. Like the Pantheon, my outsides were finally matching my insides.

I gasped. That was it! The main idea for my last essay!

I started typing. And the words flowed. Slowly, maybe, but they flowed. And flowed.

As I wrote about the experience of Rome with Vivi, my feelings about the city—and my favorite person in it—poured out onto the blank page, filling it with my thoughts, my emotions, my perspective.

And it felt good.

Ms. Morris, Ms. Deblasio, and Mr. Franklin,

This morning, instead of tourist places, my friend Vivi took me to two of her favorite locations in Rome. One is a secret garden that was really beautiful and one was a bookstore, one her father used to sit in to dream big dreams and think big thoughts. I could see why—it is full of ideas and possibilities, with all those books. I felt inspired in there, too.

Then this afternoon we saw Piazza Navona. Along the center, there are three big fountains (always more fountains!) with Baroque-style statues created by the famous artist Bernini. The middle fountain is the biggest, with four figures who look like they're on steroids representing four famous rivers, for the four corners of the world.

We also spent time at a newer museum that lets you

see part of the archeological dig of what is under the Piazza . . . that space used to be a stadium where they held the Olympics! As time passed, ground layers built up from flooding, and so that old part of Rome is buried sixteen feet under the ground. They've dug out enough from beneath the piazza so people can go see the old parts under there. How crazy is that?

The emperors assumed Rome would stay in power forever. And though it's not an empire anymore, Rome is still here, full of people enjoying life today. In fact, what I really liked about this piazza was how so many people were just hanging out, soaking in the beauty and all that history.

I'm realizing just how much I've worried about fitting in and being afraid of missing out. But here, I see people—old people, young people, and everyone in between—spending time with family and friends and just . . . relaxing. Right there in the moment. History is literally under their feet and on every corner, but they are also enjoying the NOW. I think we need to do more of that. Maybe Rome can teach us how. I think I'm finally ready to learn.

Here's a poem I wrote about Piazza Navona. I call it "City Bones."

Below my feet
There are bones
Of old buildings

That once stood
Tall and proud

They are beautiful, but
You cannot live in the past.
Those old roads are buried deep.
They cannot lead you forward.
But life is sweet like candy, if you stop and taste it.
It's the only way
To find your way back home.

So that's it. There's something about being in such an ancient city that really helps put life into perspective. And I think that can be a good thing.

Sincerely,

Lucas

There. That was all me. My work would show my full heart, even if some didn't like it. I'd be brave. Just like Michelangelo.

Over the next two hours, I pieced together my older entries. My keys clacked away as I remembered my limerick about the bookstore and the little poem about the fried artichoke leaves. I uploaded a bunch of pictures—and they were all solid, not a single toilet seat or nose-picking statue among them. And I wrote a very special final entry.

I felt good about my project. I mean, my eyelids felt like they were made of cement, but inside, I felt lighter. My family was right. I had a lot of feelings and thoughts that were about more than soccer. And I could share them.

My words counted, too.

I couldn't wait to tell Kei I'd finally finished my project. Then I remembered the fight. *Oh yeah.*

That sucked.

But you know what? If I could finish my project, I could figure out what went wrong with Kei and fix it. There had to be some misunderstanding. And I could make things better with Vivi and her dad, too. I just needed to think of how.

I clicked *send* on my project at 11:55 p.m. And then I fell asleep with a smile on my face.

I woke to my computer ringing. It was still dark out, and the clock said five a.m. Ugh.

My brothers were each snuggled up next to me, crammed into the bed. I didn't mind. Their soft snores were homey and familiar. Bleary-eyed, I peeled myself out from between my brothers and hunkered down in the corner with my laptop.

Kei's name flashed on my screen, waiting for me to answer. It was late Sunday there still.

I hesitated. Was he going to rail on me some more? Because if he couldn't handle me liking history and art, well, that was on him. But maybe I could figure out what went wrong.

Shaking out my hands that were somehow clenched, I clicked

ACCEPT, wondering for a heartbeat if Brett would be there again, even this late on a school night . . .

But Kei was alone on the screen. "Hey Lucas. Sorry to call so early, but I wanted to catch you before you started the long trip home."

I leaned back without a smile—I was too nervous. My palms were sweating. "Hey. What's up?"

He squinched one eye closed and spread his hands wide in a wince. "Sooo . . . I was thinking. I didn't mean to be so hard on you, you know, about your pictures and stuff."

Something shifted inside me, something hopeful, but that wasn't exactly an apology. I kept my face neutral. "Um. Thanks?"

He sighed, dropping his pose. "Don't be like that. I was a jerk earlier, I know. I was in a really bad mood, but your pictures are good, okay? And I didn't know you were almost failing. That bites, and I'm sorry."

Before I could respond, Kei spoke straight at the camera, totally serious for once, not a single joke in sight. "It's just . . . you know, all those pics made me think . . . it's not like I'll ever get to be a world traveler. Maybe you're having more fun over there. With your new Italian friend who speaks two or ten languages better than I speak the one." He looked down at his hands very studiously.

I almost laughed with relief. Vivi was right. I'd totally missed his worries because of my own. "I thought you and Brett would be practicing for the soccer team without me. And I wouldn't make the cut."

"Him?" He lifted one shoulder in a half-hearted shrug. "He's alright. But it's not like we've been friends all our lives or anything, know what I mean?"

"I do. You jerk." I smiled. Thank goodness. We were going to be okay, me and Kei.

He added, with a smile of his own, "And I know you're going to smash tryouts, but even if you don't, we've got more in common than soccer. And worst case, there's always sophomore year."

"Good point." I nodded. The air felt clear and light like after a storm. "Okay, so tell the truth, which was your favorite shot? Still the *David* toilet seat, am I right?"

He laughed. "No doubt. But the sad mom was good, too."

I thought of Vivi's insistence that all my photos were good. Really good. Then I took a deep breath. "What if I told you I took lots of others that I liked even more? I have a bunch."

He leaned back, crossing his arms with a half smile. "I'm guessing you're not talking about a john made of pure gold, for the pope or something?"

"Nope." I forced a casual grin and spoke fast to spit it all out before he could interrupt. "Some real photos. You know, for class. I wrote some poems, too. Like, full-on poetry. And Vivi thought maybe I should consider doing something with photography for real one day. Said I was really good, so I thought maybe one day . . . anyway, it's been pretty cool."

"Vivi, huh? She's really pretty." He waggled his eyebrows.

My cheeks grew hot, and I ran my hand through my hair.

"Well, yeah. But she's also this great musician, and I got totally in trouble with her dad for videoing her singing with a street busker, and I thought he was going to gut me—"

"A street busker was going to *knife* you?" He lurched forward, and his face suddenly filled up the screen.

I blinked and leaned away. "What? No, her dad."

"Not sure that's any better." He slowly eased back, wiping imaginary sweat from his brow.

I snorted. Kei could always make me laugh. Laughter was good. I updated him on the scoop.

Kei pursed his lips. "Wow. She sounds really cool. You know, I saw the way you looked at her—and she was looking back. Tell me you've at least told her you like her."

I didn't even try to deny it. "Uh. Well, not in so many words." I hunched my shoulders and turned the volume down on my monitor. The last thing I needed was my little brothers to wake up and overhear.

Kei gave a big sigh. "You're an idiot. Go tell this cool, musical girl that you're going to miss her and you want to keep in touch because you really like her. I mean, for real. Don't text that stuff, either. You should say it in person, especially if she's your friend."

"It's not hard to talk to her—about most things."

"Then promise me you won't mess this up. Even if her dad yells at you again. You'll always wonder what would've happened."

I swallowed hard. "I promise."

"International high five," he commanded, holding up his palm. We mimed slapping palms together. "Keep me posted on how things go with your grades, too. I'm sorry I didn't know how bad things were, but one way or another, it's going to be awesome to have you back! We might not be Europe, but we've got Dr. Pepper and barbecue."

I gave a thumbs up. "I'll send more toilet seat shots ASAP."

"You'd better." He paused and then pointed at me. "Oh, and send some of the real ones, too. I'd like to see them. Photos, I mean, not actual toilet seats. And some of those poems you mentioned. Over and out."

The screen went dark, but my insides felt brighter than they had in a long, long time.

He was totally, totally right.

I needed to tell Vivi my feelings for her. Time was running out.

There was no going back to sleep after that. Morning would be here soon enough. Of course, Vivi's dad had taken her phone and told me not to come see her, but maybe he'd let me give her an apology letter, and then I could tell her my feelings in person somehow before we left. Not ideal, but better than nothing.

That meant actually writing a letter. I stared at the blank page for a full five minutes. What was there to say? *Sorry, I messed up?* Well, yeah, there was that. But there was so much more.

I pushed the pen to the paper.

Dear Vivi.

No, I couldn't say *Dear*. Too formal. I threw that away and started over.

Hi Vivi.

Nope. God, how dumb did I sound—*Hi there, girl. I just got you grounded. Bet you want to go out with me now!*

Vivi, I'm really sorry.

Okay, that was true. And not too weird.

I never should have talked you into uploading that video when you said your dad wouldn't be happy. I hope he lets you out of the house before you have gray hair.

Working too hard to be funny? Maybe, but I'd keep it. Funny was part of who I was, too.

In case I didn't get to see her to face-to-face after all, I added:

And if you'll write me when I'm gone, I'd like that.

Good enough. If her dad read it first, he probably wouldn't set it on fire.

I signed my name and included all my contact information. I was folding it just as my alarm went off to officially start the day. My mom appeared in my doorway immediately, making me jump. "Morning! Congratulations on turning in your project! Have they said anything about it yet? I know they were going to grade it right away."

Jeez, she was more impatient than me. "I haven't checked, but it's still the middle of the night there, Mom. I doubt they graded it last night and posted it already." I actually didn't want to know my grade yet. A bad grade or comment might still derail me and my new hopeful plan.

"Well, we're driving away in four hours. Get to packing." She paused and put her hand against my cheek. "We love you and wouldn't change you for the world. Even if you fail. You got that?"

That new space in my heart grew a little wider. "Thanks, Mom."

"You'll miss Vivi, I bet," Mom offered, her face neutral. "She's been a good friend. Dad told me about what happened last night."

"Yeah. I wrote her an apology letter just now." I rubbed a hand on my chest and played the clip of Vivi singing again. Because I like to torture myself, apparently.

My mom leaned over. "Is that her singing?"

I nodded, and she watched the video with me until the end. "She's very good," she noted.

"Yeah. She wants to be a musician."

My mom tilted her head. "She's got the talent for it."

"Tell that to her dad."

"Hmm. I think he's very careful with Viviana. Raising a daughter alone, after two boys? But I'm glad y'all became friends. Just don't send her any toilet pictures. Or . . . you know what? Maybe she'd see how clever you are if you do."

I laughed, feeling freer than I had in a long time. "Well, we did promise to help each other become artists—"

"Wait. You . . . want to be an *artist*?" My mom sounded confused.

I sighed and shrugged. "Maybe. I like photography a lot, but

Vivi wants to be a musician for sure, traveling the world. That's why she let me upload the video. But it won't matter. She has to stay in Rome because of her dad and their family business."

"Well." My mom put her hands on her hips. "If you trust her, you'll trust that she can figure out her own life path. Just like you've got to find your own. Whether that involves photography, soccer, or something else. But it might not hurt if you told her father it was your idea."

"Make a confession?" Ice flooded my veins at the thought.

"Something like that."

"I guess." And maybe I could sign up to be skewered over a barbecue roasting pit, too.

"You might not be able to *say* what you need to him, but you could write him a letter, too. I've been watching—you've been getting really good at writing your thoughts. Give them both at once, and it might persuade him to show Vivi her letter, too. They won't be downstairs for breakfast for a little while longer."

She winked and closed the door behind her on her way out.

"Thanks, Mom!" I called. I suddenly knew just what to write.

Dear Signor Bonacelli,

Please know that I'm the reason Vivi agreed to upload that video of her singing. She only agreed so that I would submit my photographs to a contest. I was trying to support her in seeking her dreams, but she also wants to be a good daughter, and I messed that part up for her.

And I need to tell you one other thing: If you haven't had the chance to listen to her perform in person, you're really missing out. She's so talented, she could really be a star one day. And I'll miss her and hope we can keep in touch, if you'll let us.

Lucas Duran

The truth was, it had been hard enough to stay in touch with Kei, and we'd been friends for ages. But now that I saw the words in black and white, I knew I wanted to keep in touch with Vivi for sure. I never had a friend like her before. Even if that's all we ever were, that was more than enough.

I didn't have an Italian stamp, and it was dumb to mail it when they were just upstairs. The thought of walking up there made my stomach freeze, though. Her father probably wouldn't even open the door for me. But no way would I ask my little brothers to dare his wrath when I was the one who'd made him mad.

Clutching the letters with sweaty hands, I jogged up the stairs, left the notes on the doorstep, knocked, and ran away as fast as I could. I didn't even listen for their door opening. Besides, the roaring in my ears was too loud to hear past anyway.

Back safe inside my room, I wrung my hands. I thought I'd feel better, but I didn't. The rain was gone. We'd head out by lunch, and I'd finally leave the Eternal City.

No more time travel. No more magic. And I'd never get to see Vivi again.

I paced back and forth in my tiny room. *Go back up there.* The voice in my mind was getting loud. *Ask to see her.* I shook my head. I didn't feel like dying today. Her dad would let me know if he changed his mind.

I checked the room for all my stuff. Checked it again. Checked my email. Nothing. Made the bed. Flipping through my phone to distract myself, I caught a glimpse of Vivi's smiling face.

That new, expansive feeling inside me squeezed hard, like a closing fist. I was moving before I could stop myself, opening the door.

"Where are you going?" Mom asked, glancing up from her laptop with a knowing smile.

That grin told me she was on to me. She must have been paying closer attention than I thought. She'd already known how I felt about Vivi, when I'd barely figured it out myself. Maybe there were other kinds of magic in Rome besides the kind sending me back in time.

"Gotta clear something up." I pointed upward.

"Sounds like a good plan." She nodded at me. "Need moral support?"

"I've got it. But thanks." It was nice of her to offer.

My feet carried me up the staircase while my mind seemed to float ten feet above me. What was I doing? Her dad was going to yell at me. *She* might yell at me.

But I wasn't going to hide from stuff anymore. If I wanted

people to take me seriously, I had to take myself seriously, too. Kei was right—she deserved to hear from me in person.

I watched my hand lift and knock on the door. My breath echoed loudly in my head. I paused—I could still turn around— but then the thought of flying away without ever seeing her again had my fist dropping against the old wood. *Rap, rap, rap.*

The door swung open. Vivi's father stood in the doorway.

And he did not look happy to see me.

CHAPTER EIGHTEEN

Humble Pie Tastes Pretty Good

Did you know you can sweat right through a shirt in four seconds flat? True story.

Every word I had considered vaporized from my mind as Signor Bonacelli continued to stare at me in silence. "Uh. Um. Hi. Sir, I mean, I—"

Mr. Bonacelli raised an eyebrow. "Do you need something, Lucas?"

I swallowed hard. Pictured Vivi's face. "I do. I wanted to apologize in person. For the video. Sir. To you and Vivi."

My hands and pits were turning into water faucets. Nice.

He nodded. "I received your letter. She and I actually spoke for a long time last night. It was very good of you take the blame, though she insists you both decided together. And it is kind of you to speak so highly of her singing."

"It's all true. I've never heard anyone as good as her in real life."

After considering me, he opened the door slightly wider. "I

have not yet given her your letter. Perhaps you could speak in person . . . briefly. Since you will be leaving today."

He wasn't going to kill me. Breath swooped back into my lungs, and I tried hard not to gasp. If I touched the letter, it might melt from all the sweat going on.

"Uh. Okay?" I wiped my hands frantically against my jeans.

A quirk that might have been a smothered smile crossed his face, and he gestured me into his home, into Vivi's home, where I'd never been, not once. How strange was that? I'd been everywhere in the city but here, my friend's home. For Vivi, *this* was the heart of Rome.

He held out the envelope to me and I took it, praying I didn't leave wet fingerprints on it.

"Please give me a minute. I'll tell her you're here." He frowned at me. "We've got to be downstairs soon, but you may sit in the living room to talk. Briefly."

Translation: *Mess up again, and you'll be matching all those headless Roman statues.* Stone statues never fared well over the centuries. It's funny till it might be you.

"Understood, sir."

A short hallway led to the small living room. Colorful prints hung on the wall, and an old piano stood in the corner. I sat on the edge of the red couch like it might suddenly turn into a catapult and send me flying out into the streets of Rome.

Vases with fresh flowers were everywhere. The air smelled like perfume—I recognized that smell. I sniffed again. I'd thought it was the scent of gelato that clung to Vivi. But it was her flowers.

She entered the far end of the room, with a halo of light around her, no kidding. "Lucas!" she said, happiness clear in her voice.

"I brought you a letter," I said stupidly, holding it out like a cat tossing a dead bird at its owner's feet.

She rushed over, an electrifying smile blooming on her face. "Oh my goodness, I'm so glad you're here. I have something for you, too—you aren't going to believe it."

Standing so close that her scent enveloped me, she held out a little notebook, old and worn. I stared at it, speechless. I knew that notebook.

I had to gasp twice to get enough breath to speak. "That— that's my lost notebook!" The smooth surface of the notebook cover wasn't quite so smooth anymore, and the edges were yellowed. But it was definitely mine.

"Yes! I found it in my father's old box of poetry journals."

"That's . . ." I couldn't finish the sentence. My mind was stumbling at the time travel proof.

"Incredible, yes!" She hugged it and then handed it to me.

It really was amazing. Then a kinda horrifying thought occurred to me. "Did you . . . read anything in there?"

She looked offended. "Of course not! My father didn't either, for the record. Privacy is to be respected."

Whew. I had said a lot about her those last few days. Good stuff, but still.

Her eyes grew damp. "I did read some of my dad's poems from *his* journals, though! They were really good. He pulled out an old box of them when I asked about his writing—that's where I found yours. He said someone had left it behind in the bookshop years ago, and he'd hoped to return it but never saw the person again!" Her dimples flashed.

My knees felt like melted wax. "Incredible. After all these years!"

I slid it into my pocket, where it belonged. Its weight was a comfort. "I'm glad to have it back. Thank you."

Vivi laid her hand on my arm, just for a moment, before taking a step back. "I'm so sorry I couldn't get it back in time for your project. Do you think you passed?"

"You know, I think I did okay without it. Pretty good, actually. I don't know if I'll pass, but life will go on, and I'll be okay no matter what. But I really am so sorry about the video. I apologized to your dad. Told him it was my fault and everything."

"That's what he said when he told me you were here. And he said you thought I could be a star one day." Her voice cracked a little, and tears flooded her big brown eyes.

Oh, not the tears. "I'm—I just—"

She flung her arms around me and hugged me tight. "Thank you for believing in me, Lucas. And thank you for speaking to my father for me—then and now." Her hug and whispered words in my ear made everything in the room twice as vivid.

Then I remembered her father and jumped back to arm's length. "I don't think your dad's forgiven me, though." I cleared my throat.

She giggled. "Maybe not yet, but he's forgiven me. Even after I got mad! Or maybe because I did."

"I don't understand."

"After he spoke to you like that last night? About a decision *I'd* made? Ugh! I was in the hall and heard all of it. I was so angry! When he got back upstairs, I told him, *hey, it's my life and my plans and I want to study music*, and you know what?"

Wow, her eyes were flashing like fire. "What?"

"It worked. It started this huge conversation about life and hopes and dreams. I told him that how he used to feel about poetry is the way I feel about music. After he heard that, he thought a while and then said I can study music as long as I keep up with my other studies!"

She paused for a moment, waiting for a response. I had nothing. My brain might as well have fallen out the back of my skull. "*What?* You're just now telling me this? This is the best news!"

Clapping her hands, she said, "I'm going to get to sing, Lucas! He said I could perform for our customers in the shop for experience! We might even get a karaoke machine!"

Excitement rushed through me. "He's really not grounding you forever and a day?"

"He was going to, but I think we changed his mind, between the two of us. Well, I definitely pushed him over the edge." She put her hand on mine and squeezed once, making my pulse stutter.

Yeah, she had moves—she was going to take care of herself just fine.

"That's awesome! I'm so glad for you both!" Her hand was still on mine. Her hand was. Still. On. Mine. But we were talking about her dad here. Hardly romance time.

She nodded happily. "We stayed up crazy late talking. He'd set writing aside as a child's foolish dream, but he thinks he might start again. For fun. Thank you. I'll never forget what you did for me. For us."

"I'll never forget you, either." Here was the place to say it: *Vivi, I really like you.* She was beaming . . . would she stay beaming? She only said she wouldn't forget what I'd done *for* her, not that she wouldn't forget *me*.

Footsteps came from the hallway, and she took a big step back. I looked over her shoulder to where her father stood, tapping his wrist in a not-so-subtle sign that I'd worn out my very limited welcome. I couldn't confess my feelings in front of her *dad*.

Strike three. You're out.

"Thanks, Vivi. For, you know, everything. You're going to be amazing!"

Was it just me, or did her eyes dim a little at my response? It must have been my imagination.

I shuffled my way to the door. "We're eating breakfast in our room and leaving after lunch. Maybe we'll see you then?"

"I imagine so." She threw a quick look over her shoulder at her father when he cleared his throat loudly, and then she walked me to the door, whispering, "Do you think you've finished with your coin?"

I'd honestly forgotten about the palm reader's magic. I'd been too caught up in Vivi's.

"I turned in my project, so yeah, I think it's all done now. Do you want it?"

She shook her head. "The coin is yours. Congratulations on finishing your project. Best wishes to you, Lucas." She paused, meeting my eyes once more. "Thank you." And then she closed the door.

Well, I'd totally belly-flopped on telling her I liked her, but at least she'd gotten her letter. And I'd gotten my notebook back.

It was ridiculous to still feel bad. I'd been understandably distracted by reappearing notebooks and Vivi's great news. It was time to move on and be thankful for the many miracles I'd already been given this week.

Back in our apartment, I packed up, carefully storing my notebook in my suitcase. The coin stayed in my shorts pocket. I just felt better having it on me. It reminded me of Vivi.

Sitting on the couch, I opened the selfie that Vivi and I took together yesterday near all the artists, where her hair was brushing against my cheek—I remembered exactly how it felt.

Mom leaned over me, studying the photo with pursed lips. "Maybe you want to print that one before we pack the printer? It's nice. It would make a nice gift to her, too, on our way out."

Mom's sudden interest in Vivi was strange, but she wasn't wrong. I printed the photo out on our tiny portable printer and wrote my email and number on the back. I scribbled, *I'll really miss you! Keep in touch! If you ever want to visit Austin and its music scene, you'll have a place to stay.* And then I drew a heart. And erased it . . . but the faint line was still visible.

Maybe I could use this to tell her my feelings when I said goodbye, in person. One last chance.

I wanted to go down now, but my brothers needed help getting their bags closed, and my mom couldn't find her power cord . . . until it was almost time to grab lunch from a food cart and head out. With their school's holiday today, Vivi would be in the shop this morning. We headed down the stairs—I hurried ahead to get a spare minute alone with her, maybe.

Clanging pots and some kind of Italian radio filled the air. Vivi's voice lifted above all the noise like a bell, singing along.

I fiddled with the photo of us. Bad idea? Good idea? Who knew. But at least I was trying.

I cleared my throat. "Vivi?" I called, standing in front of the still-empty gelato counter. It always looked weird before swirling gelato was added to the gaping holes beneath the curving glass.

My parents stepped into the room just as Vivi did. Startled, I nearly dropped the photo and managed to stuff it in my back pocket.

"Hello!" Vivi said, looking between the three of us.

I said to my parents, "I'll be right out." *Please get the hint.*

Mom smiled. "We figured Vivi must be down here when you ran out the door like the devil was chasing you."

"Mom!" I whispered, mortified. *Oh my gosh.* I stared at the square tiles on the floor, wishing I could just drop right through them.

My mom laughed and said, "Vivi, do you think your father would allow you to join us for an early lunch? We'd like to take you out as a thank-you for helping Lucas with his project."

My head jerked up, and I stared at my parents. We *never* went to restaurants or cafés on travel days. They were always too worried about timing and missing flights.

Vivi's eyes widened and started doing that sparkly thing they did. "I'll ask!"

My dad stepped out of the hall, already speaking to Vivi's father, who did not smile as he said, "It's a very nice offer."

He looked at his daughter, who beamed up at him.

My dad gave me the slightest wink. Oh my gosh, they were helping me out. Giving me more time with her. My parents were being . . . awesome. Relief was like a cool breeze in the Texas summer heat.

Signor Bonacelli said, "I'll need you here this afternoon, Vivi, but you may go with the Durans for lunch now."

Vivi bit her lip, hesitating. "But what about the shop?"

"I've been perhaps leaning too heavily on you lately. You go on ahead. Luciano's Café is nearby and opens early." He touched her cheek. "I know it's your favorite."

She threw her arms around him, and he met my eyes over her head. I couldn't figure out what the message was there. A warning or some kind of thank-you? Or maybe he *had* read my notebook after all and understood everything?

Grown-ups. Who knew what was going on in their heads sometimes?

Either way, he was giving me another hour with her. Maybe his expression meant, *Don't screw this up.*

I'd try my best.

CHAPTER NINETEEN

The Last Chance

Vivi took off her apron and skipped around the counter. "Shall we go right away?" she asked, sounding so very proper the way she sometimes did. I loved that.

"Uh, okay!"

Dad said, "Offspring the Second and Third, get out from behind that storage bin. We've got food to eat!"

I prodded my brothers along. The picture felt like it weighed a thousand pounds in my back pocket, but I didn't want to give it to Vivi in front of everyone. Definitely not in front of my parents.

Instead, I floated behind her, pulled along in her magnetic field. My brothers walked on either side of her, guaranteeing our last hour together would be loud and not personal at all.

She took us to a little café that we hadn't been to before. "It's best for breakfast and brunch," she explained.

We headed down a narrow alleyway behind our B&B, turning left, then right, and then another quick turn that had me totally turned around—until we walked past a tiny alley.

"Oh!" I asked Vivi. "Is that the way to the secret garden?"

She nodded. "Just around the corner, but I took us a faster way."

"What secret garden?" my mother asked, head tilted.

"Oh, there's a sort of hidden tiny park up there where Vivi likes to hang out. You can see the Wedding Cake from there!"

We pointed out the big monument at the far end of the street, barely visible around the corner. Robby said, "I'm glad it wasn't actually a museum about wedding cakes. That's what I thought at first. Wouldn't that be the worst?"

My parents laughed.

Dad said, "Your mom wrote the section about that one. Loved it." Then he looked at me, adjusting his glasses. "And what did *you* write about Rome for your last few journal entries? You've been very busy."

I took a moment to collect my thoughts. "Well, we saw all the big places, but my favorite was the garden and this tiny local bookstore. It's not too far from here, either. It's really homey. It's a perfect place to sit and write."

Vivi grinned at me with such delight that a flash of heat spread over my face.

She asked, "Did you show them your poem about the Piazza? Or the photos you took in the shop?"

When my parents shook their heads, she clasped her hands in front of her chest. "Oh, his poetry is so thoughtful! And Lucas has taken such marvelous pictures! You should see them. I made him promise to enter them in a contest!"

"Vivi," I started to protest.

"I'm just returning the favor," she whispered. She winked at me, and I floundered for words.

My mother saved me from sounding like an even bigger fool than I already was. "We'd love to see them, Vivi, thank you. Lucas has a lot of valuable insights to share with others, I think." Her eyes looked a bit damp. Must be all the pollen out here, because mine were, too.

"Me, too!" Trevor shouted. "I have stuff to say, too!"

"Of course, my little man," Mom cooed and swooped him up in her arms.

Huh. I hadn't seen her do that in a long time. My dad had his arm around Robby. And that left Vivi and me walking side by side, leading the way.

My parents' notebooks were back home, packed away, like mine. In the sunny Roman air, we were just a normal family, enjoying a morning trip to a café for no other purpose than to enjoy it, like the people in Piazza Navona.

Best. Morning. Ever.

Along the way, I took a few pictures of my parents with my brothers. I didn't have enough with them in it. When we passed a red brick wall, Vivi said, "Wait! This would be a perfect spot for a family photo! Let me take it, please!"

I handed her my phone, and we lined up, arms all linked, the five of us in a row, the Duran family in Rome. The morning sun was rosy, and we all smiled when she called, "*Sorridi*! Say cheese!"

"Cheese!" my brothers shouted.

"*Formaggio!*" my parents called, the Italian word for cheese. Of course, now I knew *cheese* wasn't used like that in Italian, and told them so, but it still totally charmed Vivi. Show-offs.

Mental note: use the word *formaggio* in conversation with Vivi sometime.

The picture was perfect. Just like this moment.

The cafe was small, with round tables and booths. We slid into a booth because it helped pin the boys down and ordered the brunch, beginning with hot, buttery croissants. Conversation flowed around the table, with Vivi explaining more about Roman customs to my parents and my brothers trying to one-up each other for her attention. I really couldn't blame them.

A plate of strawberries appeared next, deep red and perfect. I'd never seen a shade so rich.

Without thinking twice, I pulled out my camera and zoomed in on one of the berries, capturing a dewy drop of water along the edge that glowed from the morning sunlight. I studied it closer and realized Vivi's image was reflected upside down in the water droplet. I grinned. An unexpected bonus. I took the snap.

Mom looked over my shoulder and made a *hmm* sound under her breath. "That's really good, Lucas."

I startled, nearly dropping my phone, and my cheeks flushed. I'd kind of forgotten my parents were sitting right there. My brain had just clicked over to noticing the image.

My dad rubbed his hands together. "So let's see all these photos Vivi mentioned."

"Oh, well—" I stammered. My skin felt too tight. I felt an urge to run away.

"No, really," my mom said. "I'd like that. *We'd* like that." She squeezed my hand.

The tightness eased, along with the urge to make a break for it. I tentatively smiled at her and scrolled through my favorites of the last few days, which were mercifully low on toilet seats and horse butts.

She and my dad flipped through my photos, and concrete slowly poured into my body as their silence extended. My brothers drew on a notebook my mom handed them, and Vivi just smiled serenely. Meanwhile, my heart felt like it was beating out through my ears.

"Lucas," my mom finally said. "These are great. Do you think we could use some of them in our book?"

The breath left my lungs. "Your book?"

Vivi squealed.

My mother nodded. "I think you've got a real eye for capturing the heart of a place. See how you've caught the older lady here with her dog? We actually spoke with her that day. Since we took her contact information, we could request permission to include her image."

"That is an excellent idea," my dad said.

They were taking my photos seriously. Taking me seriously. A huge grin broke out across my face.

Robby gave me a high five. And Vivi—Vivi just smiled like a cat with a big, fat canary.

"Thanks." I cleared my throat. "But you really don't have to do that, just to make me feel better about possibly failing this year . . ."

"Nonsense. These are fantastic. Like you." Her tone was brisk.

A bubbly warmth radiated through me.

My dad spoke to Vivi but smiled at me. "We've always said that Lucas is a man of many talents." The warmth from my face spread to my heart.

"But putting my photos out there, though?" I chewed my lip, torn. This was a great chance, but way scarier than turning something in for school. "What if everyone hates them?"

If I don't show my art, I can't be hurt.

My mom wiped her mouth with a napkin and shrugged. "Well, they might."

Ouch.

Robby spat out a bite of croissant, clearly about to charge to my defense. I put my hand on his arm.

"Um, thanks for your honesty?" I quirked an eyebrow.

She laughed. "No, I mean—people might hate *our* book and everything in it. In fact, some will, no doubt. But you can't live your life in fear of what people are going to say."

Mom and Michelangelo, telling me the same thing. I'd better listen.

Art requires courage.

My dad said, "You've got a great way of looking at the world. We've always loved that. I'm so glad you're finally sharing it!"

"Okay." I took a deep breath. "Okay, let's do it." My brothers gave me another high five. "But if I fail eighth grade, you have my permission not to use them."

Mom leaned her head on my dad's shoulder. "Know what? Even if you fail, I still wouldn't change a thing about this time together. When I first visited Rome, when I was just a little older than you, seeing the history here changed my entire world. So much so that I wished on the Trevi Fountain to come back."

Ah yes, the story of *The Time I Wished on the Trevi*. I'd heard it all my life.

She said, "It took me a long time to make it back here, but I knew I would one day. The encouragement of a stranger, really more than the wish itself, reminded me that I had the power to set my own future. Be who I wanted to be. I was hoping this trip would do the same for you."

"It has! But . . . it's also been really hard sometimes," I confessed. "Sometimes I felt like academic stuff was all that mattered, with all the time you've spent on your book." My brothers looked at their plates. So, it hadn't just been me getting that vibe.

My parents exchanged a glance, sadness written on them like a hidden code that I'd just unlocked.

My mom said, "I'm sorry you've felt that way. We probably *have* been too focused on our book, and we'll try to do better. But it's been hard for us, too. We were really excited about sharing our passion about Europe with you, but you didn't even try to meet us halfway. Well, until now."

My bite of croissant went down like concrete. Yeah, I'd

basically spent months slumped on the bench when history was all around me. My stomach twisted. That hadn't been fair to them.

She leaned forward, tapping my phone with a hopeful smile. "But seeing these pictures, I feel like maybe you understand now how we feel. Am I wrong?" Her eyes held mine.

I slowly shook my head. "I would have said I hated being here, up until last week. But now I wouldn't want to change it for anything." I couldn't keep my gaze from sliding to Vivi.

Vivi smiled at me, and a wave of happiness rushed through me. I suddenly felt generous toward my parents. They couldn't read minds, after all. And it turned out, they'd been hurt, too.

We'd just been running around, accidentally hurting each other because we weren't being honest. There was probably a poem in that. People could really be silly.

The words I needed came easily this time. "I'm really sorry. To all of you." I sent an apologetic smile to Robby and Trevor, too. "For all the times I've been a pig-headed jerk on this trip. I guess it doesn't mean much now that we're leaving, but—"

"No, it's great. Thank you, honey." My mom was blinking fast. Oh man, not the tears.

My dad cleared his throat, nodding in agreement. "What she said. Thanks, Lucas," he said. "That means a lot. You know, six months of travel for an adult is a lot shorter time than for a teen or a child . . . I think we sometimes forgot that. I'm sorry about that, too."

"It's okay. I get it. I wrote a poem kinda about time, actually.

About history being everywhere, but we need to live in the now. I'll show it to you on the plane." Vivi bumped my foot with hers under the table, a secret high five for being brave. I grinned at her.

Wiping his glasses on a napkin, my dad said, "We'd love that. You know, I'm really proud of how well you've done here—all of you." His glance included my brothers. "It was tough at times, but you've really made the most of your time in Rome, growing into better versions of yourselves!"

My throat felt tight, and I wrapped my hand around the coin, still in my pocket. My *extra* time in Rome had made all the difference.

The waitress interrupted, "That is what I always have said! Be at home with yourself, no matter where you are, and happiness will follow!"

I looked up and gasped—and so did Vivi. Green and silver hair, tattoos of hearts. The palm reader lady, right here at our table.

"Wait—" I began.

"Here's your check. I believe you have somewhere you need to be soon."

The tattooed woman whisked away.

"Be right back," I told my parents and darted after her.

The tattooed palm reader was waiting for me, right by the bathrooms. Such a weird place to have a discussion about magic, but it seemed right on brand for me.

I pulled the ancient coin from my pocket. "Will you be needing it back now?"

"Oh my goodness, no. That's for you. Do whatever you want with it, though you might find one last use for it before you go."

Running my finger along the coin's rough edge, I found myself smiling at her—I was actually going to miss that crazy lady. "You know, I have lots of great memories of Rome now, with my family, thanks to you."

"That's my job."

"But who are you? Or what are you?"

"Whatever is needed. But you don't need me anymore. Mother Rome is very pleased to call you a son."

Vivi appeared at my shoulder, having snuck away to join us near the WC, a regular romantic getaway. "Thank you!" she clasped the tattooed lady's hands. "You changed my life!"

"No, you both did that. Now enjoy your last bit of time together where all this first began." She tapped my hand that was still holding the coin.

"Can I get a picture of you? With us, to keep?" I asked her.

She smiled, looking pleased. "For you? Anything, darling."

I held out my camera and made sure to center us: me, Vivi, and the tattooed palm reader.

I paused. "Wait, what's your name?"

She pursed her lips. "You know, I don't really remember anymore. I've had so many names. That's fine with me, though. Names are so limiting."

I snorted. "Well, okay then. *Sorridi!*" I said. The flash went off, brighter than usual, and when we cleared the spots from our eyes, she was gone.

"Wow." Vivi said. "Magic never gets old."

I looked at the photo. The three of us smiled back at me, perfectly in focus. I'd never looked happier.

The food was delicious, and we didn't see the palm reader again. Then again, I didn't really expect to.

During the meal, Vivi told my mother about her favorite music shop, explained to my father more about the bookshop, and told my brothers about the time her family took a vacation to Sicily and got lost. She shifted from English to Italian as a new waiter came by and never missed a beat.

She was amazing.

Kei was right—I couldn't be an idiot about this. I would tell her I liked her before I left.

I hoped I could distract my family on the way home, maybe get a minute with Vivi on our walk back, but for once, they were completely engaged in conversation with us, just at the one time I could have used some privacy.

I wanted to reach for Vivi's hand as we traveled down the now-familiar path to the famous fountain. My fingers twitched, but I kept them at my side. The tattooed palm reader had tapped my hand, my hand that was holding the coin she'd given me by the Trevi Fountain.

Still giving me clues.

The Trevi was on the way back home. When we trooped past it with my parents and brothers in tow, I paused. My heart squeezed as I debated. We were almost back, and then we'd be rushing to get to the plane. I took a deep breath. "Mom! Dad! Can Vivi and I take a minute here? We'll catch up!"

My dad said, "We're running really short on time—"

But my mom shushed him. "No problem. See you soon. Come on boys." She firmly took one hand of each of my brothers, sending me a soft smile over her shoulder.

Warmth loosened the bands that had suddenly clamped around my ribs. She got all the Mom Points for today.

"What is it?" Vivi asked. "You must be so excited to finally get home! Especially since things with your Kei are better. And I feel sure you are going to pass your grade!"

"I'm excited, yeah, but . . ." I hesitated. The water splashed behind us, a laughing song. The square was thankfully not as crowded as usual. Maybe more magic?

I guided her by the elbow to the base of the steps and sat down directly in front of Oceanus—see, I learned plenty here and pulled out the photo of us together. It was now or never.

I held the photo out to her with a deep breath. "I printed out this picture of us together because it's how I'll always remember you, and I wrote my email and number on the back. I hope we can stay in touch."

"Oh, of course!" As she took the photo, our fingertips brushed, just a little. A smile spread across her face as she studied the shot, and she looked impossibly sweet.

"I'll miss you," I finally blurted. "I wanted you to know. And . . ." I gulped. "I really *like* you. As, a friend, but also, um, as more than a friend."

The rushed words hung in the air, and I didn't even want to snatch them back. Much.

She beamed up at me, dimples winking. "I know, Lucas. I *like* you, too, couldn't you tell?"

Really? She liked me back? Awesome, but wow, *why?* "Well, uh, that's, uh—"

"And I'll miss you, too." She took my hands in hers and squeezed. Any words I had gathered scattered again.

She continued on, not seeming to mind my stunned silence. "It's a good thing you threw the coin in the fountain, yes? You know it means you'll be back one day."

Thank goodness.

Wait.

"But I didn't do it right!" I protested, the realization snapping me back to reality. "I faced the wrong way, *and* I took the coin out!"

Pulling my hands free, I showed the coin to her, sparkling in the sunlight.

She let out an exasperated sound. "Pssh, so do it the right way this time!"

Oh! The palm reader had said I might find another use for the coin . . . wow, that lady didn't miss a beat.

Except . . . wait . . . the coin was getting hot . . . the sky was getting brighter. No! Not now!

CHAPTER TWENTY

When in Rome . . .

The shift happened faster than ever. And then I was standing next to a different girl in front of the fountain. A girl just a bit older than me, wearing a backpack, sighing at the fountain.

I knew this girl. I'd seen pictures of her. "Mom?!"

A much younger version of my mother looked at me with quizzical expression.

"Uh, I mean . . . *Mamma mia*, this is a beautiful fountain isn't?"

My mother, now a teenager, smiled and nodded. "It's my favorite."

I knew. Of course I knew.

"It's probably my last time to see it, though."

"What? Why would you say that?"

She glanced at me, apparently deciding I was safe. "My dad doesn't like me to travel. And I love my dad."

Boy, did I know THIS story. And now I was a part of it. Wow.

If I told her to stay home, to listen to him, that Rome was a big hassle, maybe we'd never come here. My life would be the same as it was: soccer, Kei, the works. I wouldn't almost fail. Shoot, I might even still fail *now,* if my teachers didn't like my project. Nothing was decided . . . but I could change that.

Everything would go back to the way it was.

Or . . .

"Well, if your dad loves you—which I'm sure he does—he'll want you to be happy. And you know what they say about the Trevi, right? If you throw a coin over your shoulder into the fountain, you're destined to return." I grinned.

She smiled back at me slowly. The ancient coin felt heavy in my hand.

I handed it to her, certain it was the right move. "This one's magical, too. So it'll definitely bring you back to Rome. Toss it in."

With a laugh, she did it. The coin flew over her shoulder, flashing in the sun . . . the loud plunk turned to a roar . . . a crowd of people jostled between us . . .

. . . and then I was blinking in the sun next to Vivi, my hand empty.

Vivi said, "What happened? You blinked that way—you traveled again, didn't you?"

"I saw my mom when she came here as a teenager! HOLY COW!"

Delighted, she clapped her hands. "What did you say?"

"She was sad about leaving the city, so I, uh, gave her the

coin and told her to throw it over her shoulder." I waved my empty hand at her.

A slow smile spread across Vivi's face. "To be sure she came back one day. With you."

I blushed and smiled. "I wouldn't want to miss it for anything. But now I don't have a coin to throw myself!"

"That's easy, silly. A coin doesn't have to be magical for the tradition to work." She pulled out a plain ol' euro coin and turned me around so my back was to the fountain.

Her hands were warm on my shoulders through my T-shirt, her face closer than usual. Her deep brown eyes had flecks of green around the very center. I hadn't noticed that before. There was so much more about her I wanted to learn.

She was saying something else, but I'd missed it.

"What? Huh?" I said, sounding super smart.

She grinned, like she knew why I'd been so distracted. Jeez, my face was on fire.

"I said, you have to toss the coin with your right hand over your left shoulder into the water. And leave it."

"That's it?" Sounded easy enough.

"Yep. And then you'll return to Rome one day." Her eyes gleamed.

"Okay, here goes."

I closed my eyes, made a wish to come back one day—*just in case*—and then smiled at Vivi. She grinned back at me while I tossed the coin. It landed with a little plop. I took a quick picture of it, nestled there among the other coins, as proof.

"That's a lot of wishes down there," she said.

"Yeah, but mine will come true." I knew it, like I knew my own name. I'd made up my mind about my future.

"Good."

That's all she said, but that was all that needed to be said. We headed back to the B&B, and this time I took her hand. My palm felt a little damp, but we didn't let go until after we stepped through the front door to join our families. It wasn't long, but it was enough.

Our families saw us before we let go, and they smiled. Even her father.

I was leaving today, but I'd be back.

After all, they say home is where the heart is, and part of my heart would always be in Rome.

Dear Ms. Morris, Ms. Deblasio, and Mr. Franklin,

Today was my last day in Rome. When I first came to Rome, I thought I'd write about pasta, pizza, and the pope. Because, you know, who doesn't like food, and the pope is a pretty big deal here.

And then I thought I'd write a lot about all the fountains and the art, because there's a lot of that here, amazing stuff. And I did write about a lot of it—way more than I ever thought I would or could. I included lots of facts and figures and stuff like that. Most of that was for you, Ms. Morris!

But looking back, you can see my pictures from the start of the trip were mostly silly. Here's a picture of a square toilet to show you what I mean. My mom will totally die that I included one here, but honestly, they still make me laugh. Which is fine! Laughter's good.

But over time, I got more serious. I'm really proud of how much I've learned and how hard I've worked on taking good photos and capturing Rome with my words. I hope you agree that I've done an A+ job.

It turns out that for me, though, the real Rome was about friends, family, and freedom to be yourself. I learned that no matter where you go, you need to be at home with who you are.

I met a friend named Vivi—she's a musician.

And I sort of met my family again. My parents are really smart professors and authors, and they're pretty cool. My brothers are boy-geniuses who also know how to have fun.

And I met a new version of myself, who, as it turns out, is a pretty good photographer and maybe could be a photojournalist one day. Or even a poet. And if I don't get to be on the soccer team next year—though I'm going to try my best—I can still do lots of cool things for my first year as a high schooler.

Like the Pantheon, there's a lot more to me than it might look like on the outside. My outside self had been sort of picked at by others who'd taken some of my shine, but they couldn't change my shape or what was inside. And I didn't even realize it myself, this trip was like the sun streaming into the Pantheon at just the right moment—it lit everything up, and now I see myself in a new light.

I know the best grade I can hope to get in your classes is a C, but this project makes me think that next year, maybe I can do better, if I try from the very beginning. And I will.

My best shots weren't of the Trevi Fountain or Michelangelo's work or even all the unique ones for class, though I'm going to be submitting some of them to contests. Because I think they are good enough to compete. I want to share the two best and most important pictures I took. I'm really proud of them.

First, this is my family and me. You can see that my parents are actually relaxed, so that's a rare moment. And my brothers are getting along and we're all happy. A lot of that is because of someone, who took this picture, who is the subject of the other best photo of the day.

This is Vivi. She's performing for the first time in public. She's the best thing in Rome, and she's my friend. She's going to be famous one day, and I'll be there, cheering for her, at her first concert. I threw a coin in the Trevi Fountain with her, and that means I'll return

to the city one day. And I never thought I'd say this . . .
but . . . I'm glad.

Sincerely,

Lucas

A+

Congratulations on passing
eighth grade!

The girl's wish floated on the warm summer air. The Irish palm reader—as she appeared to those around her in this time and place— smiled and studied the girl in the line to Blarney Castle. Kissing the Blarney Stone was said to give the power of eloquent speech, but this girl needed a very different gift of gab. The woman dipped her tattooed arm into her bag and pulled out a special necklace, one that would have a new owner soon.

Note to the Reader

All cities change over time, even the Eternal City, so there are references in the contemporary parts of the story that will change post-publication. The historical places Lucas travels are real, though I did take a few artistic liberties when the historical records were vague. More details are on my website. This is first and foremost a story, not a nonfiction text.

The Colosseum, **the Sistine Chapel**, **the Pantheon**, and **Piazza Navona** are all wonderful, and I'm thankful I was able to visit them. **Vivi's secret garden** near the "Wedding Cake" Monument is a real place in Rome, too. The bookstore, cafés, gelato shop, and exact B&B are fictional, though there are many places around Rome that are similar.

The Trevi is, as always, the Trevi, and the myth surrounding tossing a coin in the fountain to return to Rome was the inspiration for this story. Many movies and books have referenced this tradition, which I think only speaks to the power we humans give such things. In the end, the coin allows Lucas to time travel, which is magic, yes. But the changes inside him throughout his time in Rome are from the magic of the human spirit, available to all of us.

Happy Roman travels!

Acknowledgments

Many thanks go to Mari Kesselring and the entire Jolly Fish team! Everyone has been so supportive. My editor, Carlisa Cramer, helped shape this book so much—it would not be the story it is today without her. Copy editor Nick Rebman is a rock star for his patient attention to details, as is proofreader Connor Stratton. The cover is the fabulous work of Sarah Taplin, and I'm so lucky to have such a talented cover artist for this series. And many thanks also go to my agent, Alice Sutherland-Hawes!

To my critique partners, who are always so vital in the development of any of my books: I love each of you dearly. I couldn't do this without you.

And to my family, who put up with me being holed up in my office for hours: you're the best. My husband, children, and parents listened to me go on and on about this book and my sister and mother-in-law were always ready to cheer me on. Thank you!

And to my readers: I am so deeply grateful for the time you've spent with me and my characters. I hope you enjoy this one—Rome is a delightful city. Much love to you all!

Amy

About the Author

Amy Bearce writes magical escapes for young readers and the young at heart. She is the author of the World of Aluvia series, *Shortcuts*, and *Paris on Repeat*. She is also a former reading teacher and school librarian.

As a military kid, she moved eight times before she was eighteen, so she feels especially fortunate to be married to her high school sweetheart. Together they are raising two daughters in San Antonio.

A perfect day for Amy involves rain pattering on the windows, popcorn, and every member of her family curled up in one cozy room reading a good book.

You can find Amy online at www.amybearce.com, as well as on Instagram, Twitter, and Facebook

Explore more amazing places
and magical adventures in the
Wish & Wander series.

Check out *Paris on Repeat* by Amy Bearce.

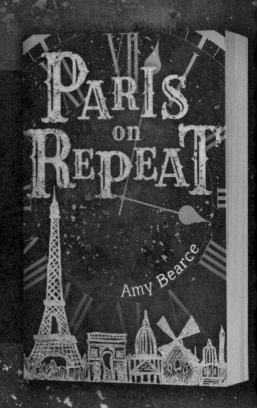

Stuck in a time loop in
Paris, fourteen-year-old
Eve Hollis has to take
big risks to discover
what trapped her there,
or she'll have to live the
most awkwardly painful
day of her life over and
over again, forever.